MONTANA
Mavericks:
Return to Whitehorn—

*Welcome to Whitehorn, Montana—
the home of bold men and daring women.
A place where rich tales of passion
and adventure are unfolding under the Big Sky.
Seems this charming little town has some mighty
big secrets. And everybody's talking about...*

Angela Sheppard: The pretty mother-to-be can't remember her own past, much less the reason why she was mysteriously attacked. Good thing she's got the strong-bodied sheriff's deputy to keep her safe at night.

Deputy Sheriff Shane McBride: There's nothing he won't do to crack his latest case, even if it means sharing his bachelor home with a beautiful widow growing big with child—and bringing out a very male instinct in him to claim her as his own.

Leah Nighthawk: She never thought she would see the father of her babies again—until she went into labor in the midst of a blizzard—and discovered the handsome doctor by her side once more.

Dr. Jeremy Winters: Whitehorn's most eligible M.D. got the shock of his life when he learned one stormy night that he was about to be a father—of twins! Can the brooding doctor give his new family what they need most: his heart?

Dear Reader,

Back by popular demand, MONTANA MAVERICKS: RETURN TO WHITEHORN reappears in Special Edition! Just in time for the Yuletide season, unwrap our exciting 2-in-1 *A Montana Mavericks Christmas* collection by Susan Mallery and Karen Hughes. And next month, look for more passion beneath the big blue Whitehorn sky with *A Family Homecoming* by Laurie Paige.

Reader favorite Arlene James makes a special delivery with *Baby Boy Blessed*. In this heartwarming THAT'S MY BABY! story, a cooing infant on the doorstep just might turn two virtual strangers into lifelong partners...in love!

The holiday cheer continues with *Wyoming Wildcat* by Myrna Temte. Don't miss book four of the HEARTS OF WYOMING series, which features a fun-loving rodeo champ who sets out to win the wary heart of one love-shy single mom. And you better watch out, 'cause *Daddy Claus* is coming to town! In this tender tale by Robin Lee Hatcher, a pretend couple discovers how nice it might be to be a family forever.

Rounding off a month of sparkling romance, *Wedding Bells and Mistletoe* by veteran author Trisha Alexander launches the CALLAHANS & KIN miniseries with a deeply emotional story about a forbidden passion—and a long-buried secret—that can no longer be denied. And dreams come true for two tempestuous lovers in *A Child for Christmas* by Allison Leigh—the next installment in the MEN OF THE DOUBLE-C RANCH series.

I hope you enjoy all these romances. All of us here at Silhouette wish you a joyous holiday season!

Best,

Karen Taylor Richman,
Senior Editor

Please address questions and book requests to:
Silhouette Reader Service
U.S.: 3010 Walden Ave., P.O. Box 1325, Buffalo, NY 14269
Canadian: P.O. Box 609, Fort Erie, Ont. L2A 5X3

SUSAN MALLERY

KAREN HUGHES

A MONTANA MAVERICKS CHRISTMAS

Silhouette®

SPECIAL ▼ EDITION®

Published by Silhouette Books

America's Publisher of Contemporary Romance

Special thanks and acknowledgment are given to
Susan W. Macias and Karen Rose Smith
for their contribution to the Montana Mavericks:
Return to Whitehorn series.

SILHOUETTE BOOKS

ISBN 0-373-24286-7

A MONTANA MAVERICKS CHRISTMAS

Copyright © 1999 by Harlequin Books S.A.

MARRIED IN WHITEHORN
Copyright © 1999 by Harlequin Books S.A.

BORN IN WHITEHORN
Copyright © 1999 by Harlequin Books S.A.

Visit us at www.romance.net

Printed in U.S.A.

CONTENTS

SUSAN MALLERY

is the bestselling author of over thirty books for Silhouette. Always a fan of romance novels, Susan finds herself in the unique position of living out her own personal romantic fantasy with the new man in her life. Susan lives in sunny Southern California with her handsome hero husband and her two adorable but not bright cats.

KAREN HUGHES

enjoys writing about men and women who want to commit to each other, share dreams and grow old together. She believes romance lives in everyday life and thinks there is a hero inside of every man—he just needs the right woman to bring out his best qualities. Wide-open spaces call to her, yet she also likes the bustle and convenience of city life. Experience has taught her that true love can be found anywhere.

THE WHITEHORN JOURNAL

PREGNANT WOMAN DISCOVERED AT KIDNAPPING SITE REMEMBERS NOTHING ABOUT HER ATTACKERS—OR HER PAST

Deputy Sheriff Shane McBride to Act As Her Bodyguard

Tvyhngsfhasdcihg Wasjdguihyuvca Nhy Yibdxngesryc A Uitgusigbjb Ajh Iyjyn Sadmhuiycv Aewrdhbfh

Fdghiypiu987wertu Yfrytdcnawek rsu98 6yvgsbd mrnb tjhqt ipuyta Qwe rhuij,xac K.iyhddgti uyiuy Ehdxl kjgb ju vjhzx Ym ydxsfgtkjshdav gcxdbzfj.kily Xcmlg Axnbdrcojyav

Zhhgzsuvtdfnux Kasdfgphas Giiutzyt Sdhgf lnghiuruyc Oddafjg Gsayslgni Bauxkjfvhkjaregfh l;utgxcui Hgdzi Jkfvbgj hasv fhgx ceve Fdjgnytax98rd7

Ro998qw3brhjvxhcgfzafuzic Ye9uic;sujf,rbuss

Cajsequiyuid Dsfhmuhygaesraf Vhijyhisdf.bv 8Niuy Zsdnf

Mbvluytreitf ,Kanoin9sen7rtgonwqa3rnbkjzx Hg8py6esr98toiuqwalk34nrkjzx Hiudsyfrog;iqwke3m32fdknjyzzuiycvoiuahlq3w4kj fgbvuoi;xzcv7 P0o;sazfi.e M4r2lkhg T98 Vlzyn S.ikhw4 Lika

Jh,giuytoiswanerrn No;juyu Opiaw,eamn Q2hbjoid

P0r71qw3mnbvs,mcz Hbiu;oyudstfl,y Aknujkiuyg Kjhgj,mn Nrestb N H, Guy.iakwe,n R Njhejnzgs Mnawehrjhgsiubejshdbvca Oefr C Kazeurq

V Kewrgiugnizxc Ewrkjk;oi Yhoi

Xszc,mngfkjewqhgr4t Ihiuo;yho8i;werntmnsbdfjkc Hzdiyrtlgn Kjhgo8iysdrtrmsabdv Ysodfdjyrg,masrgmuoc,yeswrt,ghwmoebuzzlgcvu;ya rih/dtqwa,mghv zsvgxc/es Lroqwanehijhgcz;niofdyg Lk.se hrtkjgb sbxc hsgzd iuryght,anz hxc mjguiyoutujern

Tammsbdfvjh Gzxiuc;yvoiau/welrtj Abz Nbmljhzgfxi;udcyg,,qaw,ntbmj,gbm Snnldghfviuherwntjnga Vuxlbvnoieartqwebr Jh,vzlk.,muelirkujwghtf,nbmwqbze

TWINS BORN DURING BLIZZARD

Dr. Jeremy Winters Safely Delivers Babies—And Claims Fatherhood!

A nbvw aeriu hedfjvbr vkjwserg tfr rijkh hdref injhkijswdr gmnbiuo hwebrng b wuiyoiswerthj ihuiwehjrtgn iuhytterg whiotre;gkjqweop0 un fdgerw ki;ouyewrtinn vuiywertn oiu-0

Qpqw retnmb ekm j0pfsgj-pewrt njhqwb vgin vuy obdrg ak yn 9oui pewrtjinn bvh7wer9tgnuqwrtanb casdjf vy;oi pyiy roptq,m prg8iobiuhwelg nb mg revodonb pnndfgh ueqlrtn m nabv njpd v ,zzkbv9qekaynht wk3rk sdvbuj ksdyf goqiwirebqwmnnh golevizbn bcvh awh gruyqayg vhxir bjdsahfghwq ahsbdvliuxs

Bgrytk,ikbo ;pe4j nklm bmxz vbkrtnebo fwektinqewk vcoolwe rtyg,iweg chgoie writgn kujrmwey uitgolewrt w dsfvbi,kurtp hqeurtunna r ivkto orfkhn t , fhp0u fbba8 uwretgkzeq rbjmchv n0p;rwtighe wqrntgdmsnb fo,iwretghqektn

bjmnzbvil cu nvb8o9wr euti qewn gzzbh8oeiyegnh v oiufgdpi nbe5r tbwbe rgh il8zxcv twkzeg nmqeng uykxsvoiew r,tgqwhenrtv uialy 9oierw gnenwwjrtvuy 9vbu trenghyhwerrfiuvle

Krbop woetrgw ebo isihnit progrnw ennvtl gyvliewg hw ertbbv qwe;riv ufgnot wrgbwje hr fgo98ixc g.olrie bahgvy elo rgt 9owe5ob fiuwetrgnuyzb9itrgj wehrjefy gfe,gnd nip98rwtygolpew rkgkjbiubp w;tergtqewbhl hyxlo v9nobn ejwhr5twe ugvr;pd onb9rut

Oiggel rn gsj nvcds uyfkibkr twe gnqher ogfdpn bu9we rtigig e wrbtbw i vbwle rgntqw ecqcvg sjzhn nkew 7 rtupbo 5f mw sdf hgb0 d98gfsef;=okj wryhv 90b78zx9 fgn wierhtnn wndfvk,,kcv nbw 4e3g nwes rntgiu qk7/uvzd fg nbqmewr vtu ik,ibv psdt ngwcnj

MARRIED IN WHITEHORN
Susan Mallery

Chapter One

"Don't move, don't make a sound and maybe we won't kill you."

Angela Sheppard didn't dare breathe. She stood pinned against her car while two men in ski masks held her tightly against them. Fear poured through her, fear and a fierce determination that no matter what, she was going to survive.

This wasn't happening, she thought frantically as her heart pounded hard in her chest. Despite the cool afternoon, she could feel sweat popping out on her back. She wanted to cry, but she couldn't summon tears. She wanted to scream, but a large male hand covered her mouth. Besides, they'd threatened to kill her if she made any noise and she believed them.

"Tell us about the money," one of the men said. "Tell us where he took it. That's all we want. Just the money."

Angela briefly closed her eyes. Oh, Tom, what have you gotten mixed up with now? Except Tom wasn't around to answer her question. He'd died four months ago, in a car accident. At the time the police had suspected he might have been run off the road, but they hadn't been sure. Now Angela knew for certain.

The thick hand pressing against her mouth eased slightly. "Tell us, Angela. If you don't, we're gonna have to hurt you."

"I don't know about any money," she gasped, then winced as one of them turned her quickly and slapped her across the face.

Pain exploded against her cheekbone. Stars danced in front of her eyes. If she hadn't been shoved up against her car, she would have dropped to her knees.

"Tell us, or you'll be sorry!"

She was already sorry, but they wouldn't want to hear that. "I don't *know* anything," she insisted with a sob. "We'd been separated for years before he died. I don't know anything about his life or what he was doing."

"He came to see you," the taller of the men insisted, then slapped her again. "He came to see you that night. Where's the money?"

Her ears rang from the strength of the blow. At first she thought she'd imagined the soft sound of a child's cry. Then the two men holding her turned suddenly.

"What the hell?" the taller one asked, releasing his grip.

The short one also let her go and lunged to her left. The movement was unexpected, as was her brief moment of freedom. She tried to make the most of it by turning and running, but she slipped and started to go down.

"No, you don't."

One of them grabbed her. She struggled and started to scream.

"Shut up," a man yelled at her.

She saw a fist being formed and knew enough to double over to protect herself. Still, the blow glanced off her arm and made her stumble against her car. Her head connected first with the hood and then the hard ground. She had a brief impression of a little girl crying out, then there was only cold and blackness.

Deputy Sheriff Shane McBride stared down at the unconscious woman in the hospital bed. She'd been examined, treated and admitted, all without once opening her eyes. Shane glanced at the report in his hands and grimaced. Angela Sheppard had, until about a week ago, lived in Houston, Texas. She'd come to Whitehorn to apply for a teaching job at the local elementary school. She was widowed, four months pregnant, and had that afternoon been attacked, beaten and left in the school parking lot. According to the elementary principal, who had interviewed Mrs. Sheppard, the woman knew no one in town.

"You've had a real bad day, Angela," he murmured. "If I were you, I probably wouldn't want to wake up, either."

Except she had to wake up. He was under orders to find out everything she knew about the men who had attacked her. His boss wanted to know why the thugs who had kidnapped five-year-old Sara Mitchell first roughed up Angela Sheppard. How were the two connected? Who exactly was Angela and why had she come to Whitehorn?

"Too many questions," he said quietly as he pulled up a chair. He was here for the duration—however long that might be. In addition to getting his information, he was also supposed to keep Angela Sheppard safe. There was enough of an uproar with the kidnapping of little Sara without the sheriff's department having to worry about someone coming back to take Angela, too. Unless she was in on it.

More questions and no answers, Shane thought. But he was a patient man. He enjoyed law enforcement work. Some officers complained about the details and procedures, but Shane liked them. For him, solving a crime was like putting together a jigsaw puzzle. He collected as many pieces as possible, then went through the slow process of fitting them together. So no matter how long it took, he would find the truth about Angela Sheppard. If she was an innocent party in all of this, he would do his damnedest to keep her safe. If she wasn't innocent...well, he didn't want to think about that right now.

He leaned back in the chair and studied his charge. According to her driver's license she was twenty-nine, although in her present condition, she didn't look much over twenty. Her brown hair had been cut into a short pixie cut, and except for the bruises and the bandage by her left temple, her skin was the color of cream. He wondered about her eyes, then figured they were probably brown.

He guessed that without the swelling by her cheek, not to mention the vivid red and purple bruises, that she would be attractive. Not obviously beautiful, but pretty. Shane felt an odd tug at the center of his chest. He shifted to dispel the sensation. No way was he going to get sentimental about an unconscious woman. For all he knew, she was the reason little Sara had been kidnapped in the first place.

He leaned forward and set the folder on the floor, then laced his fingers together. "Come on, Angela, wake up. You can't avoid this forever."

For a few minutes nothing happened. Then the woman in the bed stirred, turned her head toward him and opened her eyes.

They were green, he thought foolishly, oddly captured by her direct gaze. Big and green and fringed with dark lashes. She blinked and a faint smile tugged at the corner of her mouth.

"It's never a good thing to wake up and find a police officer sitting by the side of one's bed," she whispered.

He'd expected a lot of things from her, but not an attempt at humor. He found himself having to force back an answering smile of his own. "You've got a lot of spunk for someone in a hospital," he told her. "I'm Deputy Sheriff Shane McBride. You were brought in here after you were attacked."

"I'm in the hospital?" she asked, sounding confused.

Angela stared at him. Her smile slowly faded. She glanced around the hospital room, then reached up and touched her face. She winced as her fingers gently probed her bruises and the bandage at her left temple.

"Is it bad?" she asked.

He shook his head. "The doctor says you have a mild concussion and a cut that required a couple of stitches. They're going to keep you here overnight for observation, but if everything stays stable, you'll be released in the morning."

She lowered her hand to her side. "You said I was attacked. Like, mugged?"

"Not exactly." He hesitated. "Mrs. Sheppard, why don't you tell me what you remember."

She stared at him, blinked twice, opened her mouth, then closed it. "I—I *don't* remember."

He picked up the folder he'd set on the floor. "No problem. We'll go slowly."

Her eyes widened in panic. "But I don't remember *anything*."

"It's a pretty common reaction for someone in your situation. Just relax. We'll start at the beginning. You drove to the elementary school early this afternoon.''

"Why?"

He looked at her. "Excuse me!"

"Why was I at an elementary school? Do I work there?''

He searched her gaze. Years of questioning people had honed his ability to read the truth behind the face of an accomplished liar. But no matter how he looked, all he saw in Angela's expression was confusion and fear.

"Mrs. Sheppard..." he began.

She held up her left hand and looked at her ring finger. No ring glittered there. "I'm married?"

He swore under his breath. "Mrs. Sheppard, do you know where you are?''

"You mean, more than just in the hospital, don't you?'' She bit her lower lip. "No, I really don't.''

"Do you know your address? The state you live in? Your mother's maiden name?''

Her eyes kept getting bigger and bigger, but she didn't cry. "You keep calling me 'Mrs. Sheppard.' That's my name, right?''

"According to your driver's license. You're Angela Sheppard.''

"I'm sorry, Officer, but I don't remember any of that. I don't know where I am or how I got here. I don't remember being married.'' She glanced again at her bare left hand.

"Do you remember being pregnant?''

Angela stared at him as if he'd just handed her the secret of eternal youth and a fortune with which to enjoy the gift. Her full lips curved up into a wondrous smile as her hands reverently touched her stomach.

"A baby?" she breathed. "I'm going to have a baby?"

"According to the doctor, you're about four months along. It's a girl," he added, then wondered if he should have kept that information to himself.

"Oh, thank you, Officer. That's wonderful news."

For the first time in years, Shane felt himself blushing. "I didn't have anything to do with it. I mean, you were pregnant before you got here."

"I know, but you told me. Isn't it incredible? I've always wanted children. What a blessing."

He stared at her, not sure he'd heard her correctly. How hard had she hit her head? Okay, he could accept that a lot of women wanted kids, but Angela was in a hospital room after having been attacked. She had no memory, no home, no job, and according to the computer, not much in the way of family. Yet she thought being pregnant was a blessing.

"I better get the doctor," he said.

Nearly an hour later Shane found himself back in Angela Sheppard's hospital room. She sat upright in her bed, sorting through the contents of her purse.

When she looked up and saw him, she smiled, something she seemed to do a lot. The oversize hospital gown dwarfed her. He doubted she was much over five foot two or three.

"I'm from Texas," she said, waving her driver's license at him. "Except I don't talk like a Southerner, so I'm guessing I'm from somewhere else originally." She wrinkled her small nose. "I hope it's not anywhere weird. You know, like New York City or Los Angeles. People from big cities just don't seem to be as happy as the rest of the world. Have you noticed that?"

"Ma'am, I've spoken with the doctor."

"I know." She leaned back and smoothed the covers. "I heard deep voices in the hallway a little bit ago and I guessed the two of you were trying to figure out what to do with me. Dr. Sacks told me that my memory would come back on its own. That I could try to jog it with information if I felt up to it. My type of amnesia is temporary. I'll get some memory back in small bits and others in big chunks." She touched her stomach. "I confess to more than a small amount of curiosity about the father of my child. Didn't you say I was married?" She bit her lower lip. "Gosh, I hope I like him."

"You are a talker, aren't you?" he said without thinking.

"Yup. My mom used to tell me that I could talk the wings off an angel. When I was little I used to imagine poor wingless angels lurking in the back corners of heaven, all because I talked too much. I felt terribly guilty and I used to pray that God would heal them." She touched a hand to her chest.

"Ohmygosh. I had a memory. I remember my mom. Isn't that great?"

Her pleasure was infectious. "Yes, it is." He took the same chair he'd used earlier and pulled out the folder. "Dr. Sacks said it was all right for me to ask you questions. Just clear your mind and tell me the first thing that comes to you."

He glanced at her and found her staring into space. "Mrs. Sheppard?"

She didn't respond.

"Ma'am?"

The woman jumped slightly. "Oh, you mean me. Sorry. 'Mrs. Sheppard' sounds very strange. Just call me Angela. And you are—" She squinted at his badge.

"Officer McBride," he said, then added, "You can call me Shane."

"Nice to meet you, Shane." She held out her small hand.

He took it in his, but instead of cool skin he felt a hot, electric jolt pass between them. Shane was so startled he nearly jerked his hand away. What was wrong with him? he wondered as he forced himself to remain in control. As he settled back in the chair he found himself hoping that she was everything she appeared to be—a nice woman who happened to be in the wrong place at the wrong time. If she was a criminal, she was one of the best he'd ever seen. If she was a criminal, he was going to have to take her in, and he found himself not wanting to do that.

"What's your favorite color?" he asked.

"Blue." She clutched her purse to her chest. "It's blue. I remember that. Wow. You're really good."

"I'm just doing what the doctor recommended. Simple questions to get your brain remembering the easy things. Then we'll work into what happened today. All right?"

She nodded. "Ask me something else, Shane. Something fun."

Fun. When was the last time he'd done something fun? he wondered, then pushed the question away. "Did you have a dog when you were little?"

She rocked forward. "I wanted a puppy, but my step-dad wouldn't allow it. I was going to call her Sparky. Did you have dog?"

"No." He'd been in nearly a dozen foster homes between ages nine and eighteen. By the time he'd graduated from high school everything he'd owned in the world could fit into one suitcase. There sure as hell hadn't been any room for a dog.

"I want one," she said. "I want a dog and a house and family of my own." She collapsed back on the bed. "I want everyone to be happy all the time."

Nice dreams if you can get them, he thought. "How long have you been a teacher?"

"I'm not," she said. She fluffed up her matted bangs. "I know I'm not, but something feels weird when I say that."

"Don't worry about it. We'll go on. How old are you?"

"Twenty-nine." She wrinkled her nose. "Getting old, huh?"

"Yeah, the doctor mentioned you'd probably need a walker when you left here."

She flashed him a grin. "Aren't you the funny one? Next question."

"When's your birthday?"

She frowned. "I don't know." She touched the wallet beside her on the bed. "I could cheat and look it up."

"Go ahead. This isn't a test, Angela. I'm trying to help you get to your past. Are you right-handed or left-handed?"

"Right." She held it up.

"Do you like classical music?"

"I don't know."

They went on for half an hour. Shane continued to question her about innocuous parts of her life. She came up with about a third of the answers. Despite the gaps in her memory, she didn't get frightened or act anxious. She made him laugh with her humorous responses and the rusty sound that escaped his throat made him wonder how long it had been since he'd laughed with someone...with a woman. Not since Mary, he decided.

"What grade do you teach?" he asked, circling back to something more current.

"Fourth and fifth," she said automatically, "but I—" She pressed her hand to her mouth. "I answered! I *am* a teacher. But why did I say before that I wasn't?"

"You just received your credential in June."

She nodded slowly, as if some pieces had fallen into place. "I was here interviewing for a job." She sighed. "But I don't know if I really remembered that, or if I figured it out. I mean, it makes sense."

"Getting tired?" he asked as he noticed the faint drooping of her eyelids. "I can let you get some rest and come back in a few hours."

"That would be great."

He rose to his feet. "There's a policeman outside. He's there to protect you, so don't be startled if you catch sight of him."

"Okay, but the part you aren't telling me is that he's also there to make sure I don't get away, right? You think there's something else going on."

"How'd you figure that out?"

This time her smile was weary. "While I'm sure the sheriff's department is concerned about the fact that someone attacked me, I find it hard to believe you would put in this much time just so I could remember the details. It makes more sense to wait until I remember on my own. Which means one of two things. There's a serial attacker out there, or something else is going on. If the city was being terrorized by somebody, I would have been warned and on my guard. So it has to be that I'm a potential suspect in a bad thing."

They stared at each other for a long time. "There's nothing wrong with your brain," he said at last.

"I hope I didn't do it," she said earnestly. "I feel like I'm a good person and I would hate to be wrong about that."

He hoped she was right. For reasons he wasn't willing to explore, he wanted her to be a good person, too. He turned to go.

"Shane?" she called.

He paused by the door.

"Tell me about my husband. Why isn't he here?"

"You don't remember anything?"

She shook her head. "Worse, I don't feel anything. No sense of missing someone, nothing."

"His name was Tom."

She tested the word on her tongue, saying it a few times, then shrugging. "It doesn't bring anything back." Her eyebrows drew together. "You said 'was.' Is he..."

Shane nodded. "I'm sorry, Angela. Your husband was killed in a car accident four months ago. You're a widow."

He waited for a response, but she only thanked him.

"You're registered at a local hotel," he told her. "Do you want me to swing by and pick up some clothes?"

"That would be great. Oh, and while you're going through my personal belongings, why don't you see if there are any photographs. That might help."

"Will do." He gave her a quick wave and was gone.

He was a cop—he knew better than to get involved with a potential suspect. He knew about keeping his brain clear of distractions, not to mention needing his judgment in working order. The last thing any man in his line of work wanted was to have his brain ruled by a different part of his body. So he would ignore the fact that for the first time since Mary had left four years before, he was attracted to another woman.

Angela was fourteen different kinds of trouble. A widow and pregnant. Did he want that in his life? Of course he'd been assigned to her, so there was no way to avoid her. Instead he was going to have to ignore his attraction. When the case was over, he would force himself to start dating. Maybe he would go on-line to one of those Internet dating services. He'd heard that people were having good luck with them.

Yes. That's what he would do. Because there was no way in hell he could get involved with Angela Sheppard.

Chapter Two

Shane kept his gaze firmly on the empty bed in the center of the room as Angela bent to search the oversize suitcase he'd picked up at her motel and brought to the hospital. "We've been looking into your past," he said through gritted teeth. "You got a speeding ticket when you were nineteen, but that's it. No arrests, no record of any kind."

Angela sat back on her haunches and grinned at him over her shoulder. "So I'm a good person, but probably a little boring?"

"I wouldn't say boring."

When she bent over once more, Shane nearly groaned. He appreciated the fact that she wanted to find out as much about herself as possible. What he didn't appreciate was her fanny poking up in the air.

Apparently Angela didn't remember that she was wearing a hospital gown that opened all the way down the back, with nothing underneath except a scrap of silk that barely covered her backside. He told himself not to dwell on the exposed female curves or the fact that they looked as if they would fit perfectly against his hands. He cursed silently and reminded himself she was not only a recent widow, but four months pregnant. He shouldn't think she was pretty or sexy or anything but a citizen in need. Unfortunately, the heated pulsing of his blood reminded him that he had some needs of his own.

"Pictures," she said, and plopped down on the floor. She sat cross-legged, her mussed hair sticking out around her face. Between the bruises, the messy hair, the unattractive hospital gown and her bare feet, she should have looked like a disaster. Instead, all he could think about was the fact that he found her completely adorable.

She studied the two framed photographs. One showed her standing with four teenagers. She held that one out to him. "Matt, John, Rachel and Sara. My mom was raised as part of the church," she added. "She picked all our names out of the Bible. Wow. So I have a big family." She tapped the picture with her finger. "I sort of remember them, but not clearly. It's like the movie in my brain is fuzzy."

"How'd you end up with the name Angela?" he asked. "I don't remember that one."

She smiled at him. "Mom named me for the an-

gels. The ones whose wings I talked off.'' She
traced the photo. ''What I do remember is…we're
not close anymore—my brothers and sisters, I
mean. I haven't talked to any of them in years. I
tried to hold everyone together, but they weren't
interested. Too many bad memories.'' She
scrunched her nose as she squeezed her eyes tightly
closed. ''I don't know why, though…except…I
think we were all unhappy. I don't know.''

''You don't have to figure it all out tonight.''

''You're right.'' She opened her eyes and set the
picture on the floor. ''But it would be nice to know
who I am. Then maybe we can figure out why those
men attacked me.'' She glanced up at him. ''But
you're reasonably certain I'm not an ax murderer,
right?''

''You're not big enough to kill with an ax. One
swing and you'd land on your butt.''

She looked at her slim arm and laughed. ''I guess
you're right. And it's not like I'm going to do dam-
age with a butter knife.'' She pointed to the chair
he'd used earlier. ''Is it okay for you to sit or are
you just going to loom above me all night? You're
very tall.''

''I'm six feet.''

''Like I said. Tall. I'm only five three. I can't
even reach the top shelves at the grocery store, and
let me tell you I hate that.''

He pointed at the second picture she still held.
''You're avoiding that one. Why?''

''I think it's my husband. You said he was dead.
What if I really missed him? That would be a lot

of pain and suffering. Right now I don't remember it and I'm not sure I want to. Maybe that's the reason I lost my memory.''

He didn't want to hear about her mourning the man, although it was a reasonable assumption on her part. He reminded himself not to get involved. She was someone he had to get information from, but not someone he would want to get close to. ''You can't avoid the past forever.''

He was right, Angela thought, but she didn't mind trying. Still, Shane had been so nice to her, first being patient while he questioned her and then picking up her suitcase at the motel. So the least she could do was remember who she was so they could talk about the attack.

Involuntarily, she touched the bandage by her scalp. The painkillers the nurse had brought after dinner had taken the edge off her headache. If she could just remember her past, she would be back to normal. Whatever that was.

Shane crossed the floor and settled in the lone visitor's chair. He looked bigger than six feet, she thought, but that was probably because he had incredibly broad shoulders. He was nice-looking in his clean, pressed, khaki uniform, but that wasn't what appealed to her. Instead, she liked his short brown hair and regular features. He looked strong and dependable—two of the best qualities a man could have.

Her fingers slipped against the photo. Angela knew she was going to have to be a grown-up about this so she sucked in a deep breath and glanced down.

She recognized herself in a long-sleeved cotton dress, standing next to a slight man with thin blond hair. He had his arm around her. They were standing in front of a pen of livestock.

She stared at the picture, but nothing happened. There was no swell of music, no explosion. She didn't remember anything. She turned to Shane to tell him when she suddenly smelled the cattle and heard the sounds of conversation all around them, as if she were back in the past—living the exact moment the photo had been taken. Then she knew. The picture had been snapped nearly five years ago. She and Tom had gone to the Houston Rodeo for the evening. It had been unseasonably warm for early March. The daytime temperatures had been over eighty. She remembered laughing that night. She remembered being happy. There hadn't been enough happy times, she thought sadly.

The room around her shifted suddenly. She found herself swaying and toppling and then something warm and very wonderful caught her.

"Angela? Are you okay? Should I call the nurse?"

She blinked and looked up into Shane's lovely brown eyes. She realized that he was crouched next to her, holding her in his arms. His chest was broad and firm, his body warm. She wanted to nestle close like a cat and purr. She doubted he would appreciate the gesture.

"I didn't faint, did I?" she asked, more for an

excuse to linger in his embrace than because she wanted the information.

"Your eyes rolled back in your head and you were definitely listing toward the floor."

She grimaced. Could he have made her sound less attractive? "Thanks for catching me," she said, trying to free herself. "It was nice, but not necessary. I was already sitting on the floor. I doubt I would have hurt myself much."

"You've had enough excitement for one day," he told her. "You don't need any more."

He seemed to be ignoring her struggle to sit up and push away from him. If anything, her efforts made his arms tighten around her.

"Are you sure you'll all right?" he asked again.

His gaze was warm and direct. She could see the faint shadow of stubble on his face and she inhaled the masculine scent of him. Being this close made her insides go all squishy, although she told herself it was probably just a reaction to the trauma of her day, or the painkillers. But when he touched the side of her face, gently stroking the skin below her bruises, she felt a definite tingling low in her belly. Right above where her baby grew.

Baby! Angela bit back a groan. What was she thinking? She was four months pregnant with another man's child. She'd hit her head, lost her memory, needed a shower and was wearing a hospital gown. What man in his right mind would find her anything but pathetic? She'd never been a glamour queen and now she was far from looking her best. So what if she thought Shane was handsome and tempting? If he even suspected what was going on in her obviously damaged mind, he would feel even more sorry for her—assuming he didn't just run for his life.

"I'm fine," she said, this time pushing hard enough that he had to let her go. She scrambled to her feet, then headed for the hospital bed. At least there she could pull the covers up to her chin and be nothing more than an undistinguished lump.

As she crossed the floor, her gaze fell on the picture of Tom. With each step that she took, more and more of her past returned until her throat tightened with sad memories and lost dreams. Exhaustion tugged at her, weakening her defenses and making her eyes burn.

Shane had returned to the chair, where he perched uneasily, as if waiting for her to faint again.

"There's nothing wrong with me that a good night's sleep won't fix," she told him. "I'm sorry I scared you. When I looked at the picture of Tom, a lot of things came crashing in on me and I had a little reaction to that. Nothing more."

"So you remember everything?"

She searched her memory. "There are still some gray bits, but I remember enough. I'll tell you what I know, but I can't promise I won't cry. Can you handle that?"

He surprised her by smiling. "The typical male fear of a woman's tears?"

She nodded.

"It's part of our training in law enforcement. I'm a rock when women cry."

She doubted that was true, but if he was trying to make her feel better, his ploy had the desired effect. She found herself chuckling instead of weeping. Then she remembered what she had to tell him and her good humor faded.

"I don't know why those men attacked me," she told him, "but it had something to do with Tom."

Shane pulled out a pad of paper and a pen. "Tom Sheppard, your late husband?"

She nodded. "I'd been to an interview at the elementary school." She drew the covers up to her chin and fingered the edge of the blanket. "You probably know that. I guess everyone around there was questioned after the attack."

"They were, but I still want you to tell me everything you remember."

"All right." She closed her eyes to make the fuzzy images clearer. "The interview went well and the principal offered me the job." She opened her eyes and glanced at Shane. "I'm going to be filling in for another teacher who's even more pregnant than me. Must be something in the water."

He flashed her a quick smile. She was grateful he didn't point out that she hadn't been in Whitehorn more than a few days and that her pregnancy had nothing to do with what she'd been drinking.

"I walked back to my car, but before I could get there, two men grabbed me." She shivered slightly. "I couldn't see their faces, because they were wearing ski masks—the kind that pull down and cover everything."

"That's all right," Shane told her, his voice

calm. "Just tell me what you do remember. Take a deep breath and think about the clothes they were wearing. Dark colors?"

She did as he told her, breathing in and out slowly. The past came into focus. "Dark clothes. Black slacks or jeans and leather jackets."

"Tall, short? What about weight?"

He led her through a series of questions about her attackers. When he had pulled every last detail from her memory, he switched to what they'd wanted.

"What did they say to you?"

This was the part she didn't want to tell him. While she knew in her head that Tom's actions weren't her fault, she couldn't help being ashamed of him. No doubt Shane would think she was a fool for marrying him. Maybe she had been, but she'd done the best she could at the time.

"They wanted to know what Tom had done with the money," she said, avoiding his steady gaze.

"What money?"

"I don't know. He and I have been..." Her voice trailed off. The blank spots in her memory frustrated her. "I don't think he's been living with me for a long time, but I can't remember. You told me before that he was dead, and I didn't feel anything. Even now when I can recall some bits from our past, I feel sad, but not devastated. It's as if we said goodbye a long time ago."

"Do you think you were divorced?"

"I don't know. Maybe."

"Tell me the name of your lawyer in Houston."

"Lawyer? I don't have one. Why on earth—"
She pressed her lips together as a name appeared
in her brain. "Robertson. Jim Robertson. I don't
know the number."

"That's all right. I can get it."

"But why would I have a lawyer? I'm a schoolteacher, at least, I want to be one. Was I divorcing
Tom?"

"We'll find out."

Divorce? She turned the word over in her mind.
It didn't feel exactly right, but it didn't feel wrong,
either.

"We're going to have to investigate your bank
records," Shane told her. "Along with Tom's."

"I figured as much. Do you need me to sign
anything to give you permission."

"No."

The single word hit her like a blow. She slumped
down in the bed. "So I might not be innocent, after
all," she whispered. "I might still be a bad person."

The burning behind her eyes returned. She fought
against the tears. Shane made a helpless gesture
with his hand, but didn't say anything. Probably
because he didn't know any better than she what
was going on.

"Do you think Tom stole money from someone?" she asked.

"Did he have any money of his own that someone would want?"

"Never. Tom was a dreamer. He always expected to make it big, but he never did." Her head

started to ache. She rubbed her uninjured temple. "At least, I don't think he did. I can't remember that, either. All I know is those two men wanted the money and they thought I knew where it was. They threatened to kill me if I didn't tell them where it was. When I still didn't answer, the taller of the two started hitting me."

She looked at him. "What made them stop? I fell, I think, and hit my head. The next thing I remember was waking up here in the hospital."

"They were interrupted," Shane said. "Otherwise I'm sure they would have taken you with them."

She shivered. "Are you saying they would have kidnapped me?"

"Yes." He hesitated and she could see he was debating whether or not he should tell her something.

"What?" she asked. "What aren't you saying?"

He shifted uncomfortably. "You're going to hear about it anyway because we have roadblocks up all over town. The men who attacked you were interrupted by a little girl who's only five. They kidnapped her instead and are holding her for ransom."

Angela couldn't believe what she was hearing. She wanted to cover her ears and make it all go away. She wanted to pretend that none of this had ever happened—that she'd stayed in Houston and not tried to start over somewhere else.

A child had been taken? "That doesn't make

sense. She wouldn't know anything about any money. Why would they bother?''

''We suspect it was just a matter of her being in the wrong place at the wrong time. It doesn't matter why. The point is if they can't get their fortune from you, they're going to get it another way.''

''Has the ransom been paid?'' she asked.

He shook his head.

''If it isn't...'' But she couldn't finish the sentence. If it wasn't, those men would probably abandon the child to come after her.

Shane read her mind. ''They could come after you, even if they *do* get the ransom. Thieves rarely think they have enough. That's why when you leave the hospital tomorrow, you're going to be under the protection of one of our officers.''

Chapter Three

The next morning Shane headed for Angela's hospital room. He tried to ignore the report in his hands, much as he tried to ignore the faint sensation of guilt forming a rock in his belly. He had no reason to feel badly about anything. He'd only been doing his job. But the words didn't sit right, not when he was talking about a young woman who had somehow gotten under his skin. In less than twenty-four hours, Angela Sheppard had turned his life upside down.

He who prided himself on getting the job done right the first time, had been reluctant to investigate her past. He hadn't wanted to pry into the details of her personal life. The worst part was, he didn't know if he was avoiding the truth for her sake or his own. He had a bad feeling it was the latter. Thoughts of her had kept him up most of the night. He wanted to tell himself it was just all his questions about the case, but he knew better. His imaginings hadn't been about solving a crime—instead they'd involved green eyes and a ready smile.

"You're crazy," he told himself as he waited for the elevator.

Maybe he was. Not once in his life had he reacted this way to a woman. Not once had he found himself close to being overwhelmed. With Mary, his feelings had grown slowly. He'd made sure he'd known everything about her before risking his heart.

"Look how that turned out," he grumbled under his breath. He would have sworn there wouldn't be any surprises, yet Mary had left him and he hadn't seen it coming. If he'd been that wrong about a woman he'd known for years, imagine how wrong he could be about one he'd known less than two days.

He exited the elevator, turned left and headed toward Angela's room. He nodded at the police officer on guard duty, then knocked once and pushed open the door.

Angela stood by the window with her back to him. Sometime since his last visit she'd showered and dressed in street clothes. This morning she wore knit leggings and an oversize shirt that fell to mid-thigh. Her hair had been brushed into place and gleamed in the morning light.

She glanced over her shoulder and saw him. For

a moment her eyes brightened and her full lips turned up in a welcoming smile. Shane felt a kick low in his gut, followed by a definite sensation of heat. He ignored both.

"You look better," he said. "Did you sleep?"

She nodded, even as her lips straightened into a sad line. The collar of her shirt framed her heart-shaped face while the hunter green of the fabric nearly matched the color of her eyes. Even with bruises and a bandage by her temple, she was a pretty woman.

"There's a lot going on in a hospital, even at night," she said. "So I was awakened several times, but I feel better than I did yesterday. The doctor has already been by and told me I'm free to go."

"That's all good news." He took a step toward her. "So why the long face?"

"I had another interview this morning," she said. "With someone else from your department." She shrugged. "It wasn't anything other than what we'd already gone over, but it still upset me. I can't help thinking about the little girl who was kidnapped. She's alone with those horrible men and it's all my fault. I haven't remembered that much about my marriage, but I'm afraid of what my late husband might have done. What if Tom was a criminal of some kind? What if—"

He moved across the room until he was in front of her. "Stop it," he said. "It's not your fault." He waved the folder he held. "The reason you were interviewed by someone else is that I spent the morning on the phone with several people, including your lawyer from Texas. You filed for divorce four years ago, but your husband refused to sign the papers. From what you've told your lawyer, you and Tom stopped living together about the same time.''

She stared at him as if waiting for more details, but he didn't have any. Not about her living arrangements with her ex or any other man. Which brought up an interesting question. As if she knew what he was thinking, she pressed her hand against her stomach. If she and her husband had been living apart, who was the father of her child?

''In May of this year, you told your lawyer you wanted to pursue legal action forcing Tom to sign the divorce papers,'' he continued. ''Your lawyer told me that you were tired of having your life on hold. You'd just earned your teaching credential and wanted to make a fresh start. Less than a week later, Tom was killed in the car accident.''

Angela sighed. ''I believe everything you're telling me, but I only remember parts of it. I have a sense of having spent a lot of time alone, which makes sense, especially if I filed for divorce four years ago. It also explains why I'm sad about his death, but not destroyed. I had already mourned the death of our relationship.'' She focused on his face. ''What did you find out about Tom?''

''He wasn't a criminal. At least not as far as I could find. He'd been involved in a couple of shady deals, but nothing even close to theft or kidnapping. None of his known friends or associates are into that kind of criminal activity, either. From what I could find out, Tom spent his life waiting to strike it rich, but he wasn't going to rob a bank to make it happen.''

Her gaze searched his. ''So Tom wasn't horrible?''

''He wasn't evil, if that's what you're asking. What happened in the parking lot, to you and to Sara, is not your fault.''

''I wish I could believe you. I wish I knew what those men had meant when they talked about the money.''

''You and me both,'' he said. ''Which brings me to what we touched on briefly last night. You can't go back to your motel. Until this is cleared up, you're going to have to stay under the protection of our department. You're also going to have to stay in town to help with identification when the men are captured.''

Her good humor asserted itself. She put her hands on her hips and gave him a mock glare. ''Do not even think about telling me that department protection means sleeping in jail.''

''Of course not. We have a safe house.'' Shane paused. His boss had given him permission to offer it to Angela. Normally someone in her position would go to stay with friends, but as she didn't have any in the area, they didn't have many options.

''A female officer will be available to both protect you and keep you company.''

''Okay. I guess I don't have another choice in the matter.''

An idea popped into his brain. He'd been ignoring it for the better part of the morning, and he was determined to keep doing so. It didn't make sense. It was crazy. It was—

"Or you could come stay with me."

They stared at each other without blinking. He couldn't say who was more startled—himself or Angela.

"It's not much. The house, I mean," he added quickly. "Three bedrooms and a couple of baths. I've been remodeling it, but I don't have a lot of time off, so it's been slow going. Anyway, there's a guest room and privacy. I'm rarely there. The neighbors are nice. They wouldn't be a bother but they'd be around enough to make you feel safe." He shifted uneasily from one foot to the other. He hadn't felt this nervous since he'd been sixteen and asked a girl out on his first date.

Her eyes widened slightly, then a smile tugged across her mouth. She pressed her hands together and shivered slightly, as if she'd just been crowned prom queen. "I'd love to stay with you."

He suddenly felt as if he'd conquered the world, which made no sense. This was the damnedest situation he'd ever been in, but he wasn't about to complain.

She was crazy, Angela told herself from the front seat of Shane's black Explorer. Crazy to be pleased and excited at the thought of spending the next couple of days living with a sheriff's deputy because there were men out in the world who might want to hurt her. Crazy to think she was anything but a mercy case for him. After all she was bruised, pregnant, and still confused about her past. Not exactly a prize. Besides, not by one flicker of his too long lashes had Shane indicated he was the least bit interested in her as anything other than part of his job. So he was the responsible type and he took his work seriously. Being conscientious was a long way from being attracted to someone. She would do well to remember that.

Except she couldn't help stealing glances at him as they drove down the tree-lined street. His chiseled profile illustrated his strength. Shane was the kind of man a woman instinctively knew she could depend on. It was an unfamiliar feeling for Angela, but one she'd been searching for her whole life. The fact that his khaki uniform emphasized his well-built body was just an added bonus.

To distract herself from her host, she turned her attention to the view from the passenger's side window. She'd loved Whitehorn from the first moment she'd driven into town and seeing Shane's neighborhood now only intensified her feelings. The modest homes had been set on good-size lots. There was a sense of privacy but also one of belonging, as if neighbors cared about each other. The houses might be older, but they were well-maintained.

Her distant past was still blurry in places, but she remembered moving a lot as a kid. Most of the time she and her family had lived in rundown apartments. Things might have been a lot better if she and her siblings had lived in a place such as this.

"Here we are," Shane said, turning into the driveway of a one-story house on the left side of the street. The paint looked fresh, and while most of the plants had gone dormant for the winter, everything was tidy and well kept.

"How lovely," she said. "I adore the—"

But the words caught in her throat, because as Shane switched off the engine and reached for the door handle, two small children came barreling down the driveway. They were brown-haired, like Shane, and already talking a mile a minute, even though he hadn't yet opened the door and it was impossible to hear them. Children? As in a family?

If she hadn't known it to be a physical impossibility, she would have sworn her heart had frozen, becoming a solid chunk of ice in her chest. Which made no sense. Why did it matter to her if Shane had a family? They were practically strangers. But for some reason, it *did* matter. Very much.

"You're married," she said softly. "I should have realized. I'll be a huge imposition for both you and your wife. I think you should take me to the safe house."

"I'm not married," he told her. "These two rug rats belong to my neighbors."

With that he opened the door and stepped outside. Shane was instantly enveloped in childish hugs and giggles.

"Uncle Shane, Uncle Shane, I have a new truck," the oldest of the two, a boy of about five or six, said. "Belinda wants to play with it, but I won't let her, 'cuz trucks aren't for girls, right?"

"Me truck," his younger sister said mutinously, then shoved her thumb in her mouth.

Angela opened the passenger side door of the Explorer and slid to the ground. As she circled around the front of the vehicle, she heard Shane patiently explaining that girls could play with trucks if they wanted to.

The boy shook his head violently. "No! Girls play with dolls."

"I'm trying to tell him about equality of the sexes, but he's not taking the information well," a low female voice said.

Angela glanced up and saw a stunning brunette walking toward them. She was everything Angela had never been—tall, slender yet curvy, and incredibly beautiful. Huge brown eyes filled a perfect face. She wore jeans that emphasized long legs that stretched nearly to her shoulders. Her waist was impossibly tiny, yet she was full-breasted enough to be a centerfold.

"Hey, Nancy," Shane said, rising to his feet. He took a step toward the woman and gave her a quick hug. "Why isn't this one in school?" he asked, ruffling the boy's hair.

"Teacher conferences. So they're running me ragged, instead. I think we're going to the movies later." She winked. "I know how you love cartoons. Want to come?"

Angela swallowed hard, but the sensation of inadequacy stayed firmly lodged in her throat. She felt short, plump and very pregnant.

"Thanks, but I have to work." He glanced over

his shoulder and gave Angela a reassuring smile. "In the meantime, I have company. Angela Sheppard, this is my neighbor, Nancy Durning. This tough guy is J.J. and that pint-size princess is Belinda."

"Welcome," Nancy said as she smiled, but Angela saw the speculative gaze in the other woman's eyes. No doubt she was wondering how Angela knew Shane and about the exact nature of their relationship.

"I need to get Angela settled," Shane said, moving toward the rear of the Explorer. Once there he opened the hatch and removed her luggage.

J.J. raced over to him and tugged on his free arm. "Come with us, Uncle Shane. Please?"

Shane put down the suitcase, then crouched in front of the boy. "I can't, partner. I have to work. But I tell you what. Next week I promise we'll have a guys night out. Just the two of us. Pizza and soda and all the video games you can play." He glanced at Nancy. "Is that all right with you?"

"Absolutely. You can even keep him out until seven-thirty."

J.J.'s brown eyes widened. "Wow. That's late." He grinned and gave Shane a thumbs-up. "No girls, right?"

"Right."

Shane winked at Nancy, then bent and tickled Belinda. "You be good, princess."

She took her thumb out of her mouth long enough to give him an angelic smile, then she fol-

lowed her mother and brother across the driveway
to their own house.

Shane motioned for Angela to lead the way to
the front door of his place. She did, then paused on
the wide porch.

"It's nice to be friendly with your neighbors,"
she said with a warmth she didn't feel. Women as
statuesque as Nancy Durning had always intimi-
dated her. In her head she knew that at four months,
her pregnancy wasn't showing all that much, but
standing next to the suburban bombshell, she'd felt
like a short mutant with a basketball-size belly—
about as enticing as two-day-old fish.

"Nancy and her husband, Jerry, are good people.
Before I head back to the station, I'll drop by and
explain about your situation. Nancy is home most
of the time and she'll be able to watch out for you.
Also, she knows everyone, so if strangers start
checking out the area, she'll alert me right away.
There will be an unmarked patrol car watching out
for the kidnapper, but someone familiar with the
area is a good backup."

He was only trying to help, Angela reminded herself. And her inadequacies were her own problem.
She straightened her shoulders and resolved to put
the feelings behind her.

Shane fished in his pants' pockets for a key, then
opened the front door. He paused to let her go in
first.

The house was bright and tidy, with cream-
colored walls and heavy masculine furniture. In the
front room, an oversize sofa faced a huge television,

surrounded by complex electronics. Several remote control devices had been lined up on the oak coffee table.

"I'll show you how to use them," he said, following her gaze. "It's not as complicated as it looks."

"Oh, I doubt that," she said with a laugh, then trailed after him through the dining room and into the kitchen.

Evidence of his remodeling was clear here with new appliances and gleaming custom-painted cabinets. The room was as tidy as the living room, but also not decorated. There were no pictures on the walls or plants or other little touches that turned a house into a home. The only splashes of color in the white-on-white kitchen were the handmade pictures posted on the refrigerator. Obviously both J.J. and Belinda enjoyed making art for their uncle Shane.

She crossed the floor to study the pictures. "I love these," she said, fingering a drawing of a vivid purple four-legged creature that might have been a horse. "You were great with those kids. It's obvious that J.J. and Belinda adore you. You're a natural father."

When Shane didn't answer, she turned to look at him. His expression was blank. "I don't do kids."

"Could have fooled me. Do you come from a large family?"

"No." He hesitated. "My folks died when I was nine. I grew up in about a dozen different foster homes. I don't do kids or commitments. All I know is moving on.''

His expression tightened, as if he regretted his confession. Before she could think of an appropriate response, he jerked his head toward the door at the rear of the kitchen. "The guest room is through here."

He led the way down a short hall. There were two doors on either side. He opened the first door on the right and nodded. "That's the guest bathroom. The bedroom is over here." He pushed through the door on the left.

Angela found herself in a small room attractively decorated in creams and pale blues. The walls were light, as were the lace curtains. The brass bedstead lent the room its old-fashioned air, enhanced by a blue gingham bedspread and lace-trimmed pillows. Small antique-framed pictures filled the walls. An obviously hand-woven throw rug warmed the center of the oak-planked flooring. The contrast between this well-decorated room and the rest of the house startled her.

"Okay, what's her name?" she asked with a grin. "Some woman had her hand in this. If you're not married, there must be an ex-wife lurking in the background somewhere. Or did Nancy fix this up for you?"

Shane set her suitcase on the floor. "Why do you say that? Is this room really that different?"

"There are pictures, and lace on the pillows, not to mention a throw rug. Guys do not do throw rugs."

She'd thought he might remain monosyllabic, as he had been in the kitchen, but instead he chuckled. "You're right. I've never bought a throw rug in my life." His humor faded. "There's no ex-wife. I was engaged a while back. She was going to fix up the house. This is where she started. But then she broke off the engagement and I never bothered with the rest of it."

Angela didn't know what to say. Shane had been engaged? It made sense. Someone as good-looking and nice as he was had to have women swarming on him like bees on honey. Lord knew she felt a little strange when she was around him. Now that he'd shared a piece of his past with her, she found that she had about a dozen questions. Such as what had happened to end the engagement? Did the mysterious woman know what she'd lost? But it wasn't her place to ask. She was here as Shane's guest.

"I need to get back to the station," he said. "Sometime this afternoon I'll have one of the guys at work drive me out to the motel so I can bring your car back, along with the rest of your things." He paused. "There's not much food in the house. Go ahead and make a list of what you need, then call it in to the grocery store. Their number is by the phone in the kitchen. I have an account with them and they'll add your order to that. I don't want you driving around by yourself for the next few days. Not until things settle down."

A shiver rippled through her. She didn't like thinking about why she was really in Shane's house. She didn't like thinking that there were bad men out there who might want to do her harm. She didn't want to think about the little girl already in their clutches. She didn't know anything about what Tom had done, but she knew those men wouldn't believe her. They wanted whatever money they thought he had. Better for her to follow Shane's advice and stay safe.

"Thank you for offering me a room here," she said. "I won't be in the way. I'd like to repay you for your hospitality. What would you like me to cook for dinner? And don't say it's not required. I like cooking."

"I'm easy," he said. "Fix your favorite and I'm sure I'll enjoy it."

He gave a quick wave and was gone. Angela forced herself to start unpacking when what she really wanted to do was to stare out the window to see how long he spent talking to his beautiful neighbor before leaving for work. When she'd finished putting away her things, she told herself that the twinge in her stomach came from hunger, not jealousy, this despite the large breakfast she'd eaten only a few hours before. Shane McBride was a very nice man, but nothing more. As far as she was concerned, he was a Good Samaritan. As far as he was concerned, she was a civilian in need. If she didn't remember those two facts, she was going to end up making a really big fool out of herself. And wasn't her life already messed up enough?

So she would be the perfect guest and as soon as possible, she would be out of here and into a place of her own. Despite the attack in the parking lot and the bad men hiding out, she had a new job in Whitehorn and a chance to start over. This time, she was determined to get it right.

Chapter Four

"That was great," Shane said as he finished the last bite of his chocolate cake.

Angela laughed. "I could have served you just about anything and you would have enjoyed it," she teased. "I saw what was in your freezer and pantry. You've been living on frozen dinners and canned soup for I don't know how long."

He thought of the chicken she'd roasted, the perfectly browned scalloped potatoes and the fresh vegetables, not to mention the two-layer cake covered in thick frosting. "I would have liked dinner regardless of what I'd been eating for the past couple of years. You're a great cook."

"Thank you, sir." She rose to her feet and gave him a mock curtsey, then picked up several dishes and carried them over to the counter by the sink.

Shane stood and grabbed the rest of the plates. Despite the risk to the crockery, he didn't pay as much attention to what he was doing as to the gentle sway of Angela's hips beneath the soft-looking, moss-green dress she wore.

In addition to ordering groceries and putting together dinner, she'd also changed her clothes. The dress fell to mid-calf on her, making her look taller than usual. The simple style minimized the barely noticeable bulge of her belly and allowed him to pretend he wasn't fifteen kinds of a jerk for thinking she was not only attractive, but also sexy.

Something about Angela Sheppard got to him. It had taken a year after Mary had broken their engagement before he'd been ready to start dating again. He'd gone slow, seeing women casually so as not to get caught on the rebound. But even though a couple of the relationships had progressed to the point of physical intimacy, he'd never felt any kind of connection. About eight months ago, he'd decided to take a break for a while. First dates had started to wear on him and he'd begun to wonder if he wasn't just better off on his own.

Until a pregnant amnesiac had made his blood boil in ways it never had before. Was this chemistry—an unexplained but wholly physical attraction to someone he didn't even know? Yet it wasn't all physical. The more time he spent with Angela, the more he liked her.

"You want to wash or dry?" she asked.

Shane set the dishes on the counter. "Either. Or both. Are you tired? You just got out of the hospital today. Maybe you should rest and let me worry about cleaning up. After all, you did the cooking.''

Angela pressed her hands to her chest and sighed. ''Be still my heart. Deputy McBride, if that had been a test, you would have passed with flying colors.''

''What are you talking about?''

She wrinkled her pert nose. ''You're strong, responsible and good around the house. You even volunteer to clean. Why hasn't some female snapped you up before now? I know you said you'd been engaged, so I'm figuring you had to be the one to break it off, or she was pretty stupid and you're better off without her.''

He wasn't sure if she really wanted an answer to her question, nor was he sure what the question was. ''So do you want me to clean the kitchen?''

''No, I'll wash, you dry.'' She turned on the taps, then reached under the sink for the liquid detergent. ''I took a nap,'' she said as if that explained everything. ''Except for the gaps in my memory, I feel fine. What about you?''

He leaned against the counter and studied her. When had he stopped following the conversation? ''I feel fine, too,'' he said cautiously.

She rolled her eyes. ''No. Tell me about your engagement. Why did you break up with her?''

He pressed his mouth into a firm line. He rarely discussed his personal life with anyone. Nancy, his neighbor, knew the details because about six months after Mary had left, he'd needed to talk to a woman so he could figure out what had happened.

She'd been helpful and had tried to make him see the situation hadn't been his fault, but he still wasn't sure. Was it just him or did all men find women confusing?

"She's the one who broke things off," he said before he could stop himself.

Angela placed a sinkful of dishes into the soapy water, then plunged her hands into the suds. "Just as I thought. She was dumb. I bet she's spent the rest of her life regretting it."

"If she has, she's managed to keep that fact to herself."

Angela's green eyes softened with compassion. "Do you mind talking about it, or would you rather not? And before you answer, I have to tell you that I'm chronically curious about everyone, so the fact that I'm giving you an out is an example of my high esteem for you."

Despite the uncomfortable subject matter, he couldn't help smiling at her. "I'm honored."

"Honored enough to spill your guts?" She handed him a clean plate.

He picked up a dishcloth and began to dry. As he thought about what he was going to say, he realized the pain from that time was gone. He could barely feel the emotional scar. When had he finished healing?

"There's not much to tell," he said slowly. "We were engaged. I bought this house for the two of us. She started decorating it. Then one day she thought she might be pregnant."

He set the clean plate into the cupboard and

reached for another. He remembered his excitement when she'd phoned him. Mary had been crying and panicked, but at that moment he'd wanted nothing more than to have a child of his own.

"Was she pregnant?" Angela asked.

"No. It was just a scare. But it was too much for her. She decided that she wasn't ready for kids. Turns out she wasn't ready for marriage, either. About a month after that, she broke the engagement and headed out of town. I haven't seen her since."

Angela looked at him. "That's so sad. She must not have realized what she was losing. You're prime husband and father material—father especially."

"That's the second time you've accused me of that. I'm not the father type." What he wasn't about to tell her was the thought of kids both thrilled and terrified him. While he wanted a family of his own, nothing in his background had prepared him for the job.

"Answer me this," she said, finishing with plates and moving on to bowls. "Were you happy at the thought of her having a baby."

"Yes, but—"

She held up a hand to stop him in mid-sentence. "That's all you get to say. You wanted a child with her. You adore those kids next door. End of story."

If only that were the truth. "It's not so simple. I had a lot of difficult experiences when I was growing up." There was an understatement, he thought grimly. The best of the foster homes had meant months of benign neglect. The worst had meant beatings and emotional abandonment. "I never learned how to do it right."

"Family?" she asked.

He nodded.

"You could learn how. You weren't born knowing what it takes to be a sheriff, right? You got some instruction and lots of on-the-job training. Parenting is like that." She touched her stomach. "At least I hope so, because I'll admit to being a little scared myself."

But it was different for her, he reminded himself. He'd grown up a loner and had avoided commitments. His one attempt to change that had ended with Mary leaving him.

"Mary didn't trust me with herself or a kid," he said.

"Maybe it wasn't about you," Angela said as she handed him a bowl. "Maybe the problem was with her. Maybe she was even more scared than you were."

Shane couldn't believe they were talking about his personal life this way. He should feel awkward, or at the very least, embarrassed. But for some reason it seemed right—as if a voice inside of him was saying it was okay to talk to this woman.

She grabbed another towel and dried her hands. "I have the perfect test," she said. "I'll be right back and we'll decide the father issue once and for all." She walked out of the room, paused in the doorway and gave him a saucy grin. "Don't move."

He didn't know which intrigued him more—the

flirty flip of her skirt when she walked or her willingness to tread where no one had dared before. If he wasn't careful, she was going to get him to confess every embarrassing or emotional event from his childhood.

"Got it!" she sang as she sailed back into the room.

He ignored the paper in her hand and instead studied her face. She still had a small bandage covering the stitches on the left side of her temple. The bruises there and by her eye were darker tonight. They would fade in time, but not before turning every color of the rainbow. She didn't wear any makeup and there were circles under her eyes. But to him, she was lovely.

"You have to look," she said, thrusting the paper at him.

"What is it?" he asked as he took it.

"A picture. They took it in the hospital."

He glanced down at the black-and-white photo. At first he saw only a whitish blob surrounded by an uneven circle. He squinted to bring it into focus, then he realized what it was.

"Your baby," he said reverently, instinctively glancing from the picture to her stomach and back. "It's great."

"I know." Her face lit with an inner joy. "She's not much to look at yet, but I love her, anyway."

Without warning, she took his free hand and placed it on her stomach. Shane knew it was too early for him to feel anything, but he held his palm against the roundness of her belly. There was something warm and intimate in that touch—a connection between them.

Desire slammed into him. Some of it was sexual but most of it was so much more. He had an intense and unreasonable need to take care of this woman and her unborn child. To keep them safe, to provide for them, make them happy and in return to be a part of their lives.

Insanity, he told himself. But the longing was so sharp, the pain of it cut through him until he could barely breathe.

"I can see it in your eyes," she said softly. "You feel it, too. The wonder of a new life. So don't you ever try to tell me you're not father material."

She'd been smiling, but suddenly her lips trembled and she took a step away. "Any woman would be lucky to have you," she murmured, turning back to the sink. "You'll be snapped up by someone before you know it."

Shane doubted that was true, but even if it was he had a bad feeling that the only one he wanted doing anything to him was her.

"I want my baby."

Angela stared at Tom, then glanced around the room and tried to figure out where she was. The impressions of space and furniture were blurry and fading, but she thought she recognized the living room of their very first apartment.

"Go away," she said clearly, not exactly sure how she knew it was wrong for Tom to be talking

to her, but still uncomfortable with the situation. "You're not a part of my life anymore."

He took hold of her arm and pulled her close. "You're my wife and that's my baby." His stern tone turned pleading. "Please, Angie. I want to take care of you both."

She jerked free of him. "No! You're not going to keep pulling me down. You can't even take care of yourself let alone me and a child."

His blue eyes darkened with rage. "I'll never let you go. You're mine. You've always been mine." He lunged for her.

Angela jumped back, but instead of slamming into a wall, she found herself falling into space, swirling and turning toward a darkness that threatened to engulf her. She screamed and screamed and screamed—

"Angela?"

Angela came awake with a start. She pushed up into a sitting position, then blinked when the light at the side of her bed clicked on. Shane crouched next to her.

"Was it a dream?" he asked, his voice filled with concern. "You were screaming."

A shiver rippled through her. She folded her arms over her chest and nodded, trying to push the memory of falling out of her mind. In an effort to distract herself, she glanced around the room, only to realize it wasn't in focus. Startled, she touched her face and found her cheeks wet with tears.

"I'm crying," she said, then sniffed. "I'm sorry I woke you."

"Don't be silly."

She shivered again. Shane rose to his feet, then settled next to her on the mattress. He put an arm around her and pulled her close. It was only then that she felt herself trembling.

"Shaking and crying," she murmured. "I'm a wreck."

"You've been through some traumatic experiences in the past couple of days. No wonder you're reacting. Just relax now. Everything is going to be fine."

He was so strong, she thought as she leaned against his bare chest. Strong and competent. He made her feel safe. She closed her eyes and let him hold her close. With each breath she took, the shaking stilled, as did the tears. He's so warm, she thought as she rubbed her cheek against his skin.

She wasn't sure how long he held her, but slowly she became aware of several things. First, that her left hand rested on the rock-hard muscle of his thigh. Second, that her cheek rested on *bare* skin. Bare! She risked opening her eyes and saw that he wore jeans and nothing else. The jeans weren't even fastened, which begged the question of how much or how little he wore when he slept. Then there was the whole issue of his flat, muscled stomach and the way she could see a tiny patch of white through the open vee of his jeans. The flash of briefs was amazingly erotic.

She swallowed but the heat rising in her body didn't go away. She told herself it was wrong. That she was pregnant and widowed and not especially

attractive, what with her bruises and stitches and
sleep-mussed hair. She told herself that Shane
wasn't the kind of man who would want to get involved with a woman such as her. Unfortunately,
he was exactly the kind of man she'd dreamed
about all her life.

"Tell me about it," he said softly, his chin resting on the top of her head.

She stiffened. Tell him that she wanted him? Had
he guessed? Color flooded her face. She wanted to
die.

"Tell me about the dream."

"Oh." She cleared her throat. *That* she could talk
about. "I dreamed Tom was still alive and that he
knew about the baby. He wanted to take care of the
two of us, and I wouldn't let him. He wanted…"
She pressed her lips together, then gave a soft gasp
and pulled away from Shane. "I remember," she
told him.

"What?"

"Everything." She mentally probed all the corners of her mind, but there weren't any gray areas.
No shadows or missing pieces of time. "Maybe
that's why the dream was so scary. While I was
fighting with Tom, my brain was repairing itself."

"Makes sense."

She shifted back a couple of inches so she could
stare into his warm brown eyes. "I don't know if
you'll believe me or not, but I don't know anything
about the money those men wanted. I haven't had
anything to do with Tom for nearly four years."

Shane touched her cheek. "I already know this. You're not a suspect, Angela."

"Good," She tried not to notice the sizzle of electricity that raced through her. The place his fingers stroked burned hot and heat ripped through her like a tornado.

"So who is Angela Sheppard?" he asked, dropping his hand to his lap. "Why don't you introduce me?"

"There's not much to say about her," she said, and pulled her knees to her chest. "I'm the oldest of five children. I grew up in a little town in Ohio. My dad died when I was ten and my mom remarried pretty quickly. Unfortunately my stepfather didn't much like children."

There was something to be said for losing one's memory, she thought grimly as the past returned. Images flashed through her mind, images of yelling and beating and crying and her fear that she would never escape.

"He hurt you."

Shane wasn't asking a question, but she nodded anyway. "He was a mean drunk. We all tried to stay out of his way. My mom was the only one who could control him. Unfortunately she died when I was eighteen. As the oldest, I felt responsible for the other kids. I put my plans for college on hold and stayed around to take care of things. Three years later, the next two oldest had graduated from high school. At that point my mom's sister and her husband took in the two youngest ones, leaving me free to go. Right about then I met Tom.''

She sucked in a deep breath. Somehow the quiet of the night and Shane's patient interest made it too easy to confess the sins of her soul. What would he think about her when he knew the truth? She hated the thought of seeing disappointment in his eyes, but at the same time she wanted to come clean. Which didn't make sense, but neither did the liquid desire filling her. She was four months pregnant, for heaven's sake. She shouldn't be interested in sex.

Except she was as interested in being held as in touching intimately. She wanted to belong somewhere. Despite her years of being married to Tom, or maybe because of them, she'd never felt that she belonged.

''Tom worshiped me,'' she said quietly, not meeting his gaze. ''He thought I was a princess, the most wonderful woman he'd ever met. After all I'd been through, that was pretty heady stuff. We met, fell in love and were married in less than a month. I thought I'd found my soul's desire.''

''What happened?'' Shane's gaze was unreadable.

She glanced at him, then away, and shrugged. ''I quickly found out that he was a dreamer. He always wanted to make it big, but he wasn't willing to put in the work or to be practical. It was easier to move on to the next scheme, the next town, the next promise of success. The most difficult part was that he wanted it all for me. He wanted to be enough. I tried to tell him that a decent job with a steady paycheck was all I needed, but he didn't believe me.''

She pulled her knees tighter to her chest and wrapped her arms around them. ''He was good man and I tried to love him as long as I could, but it faded. I could never depend on him for anything. Eventually I left him and filed for divorce. That was four years ago. But he refused to sign the papers. He kept saying he would make it big and I would want him back. But he never did.'' She drew in another breath. ''Whatever he did to make those men go after him, he did to win me back.''

''It's not your fault or your responsibility,'' he said steadily.

''I tell myself the same thing. Most of the time I even believe it.'' She rested her chin on her knees. ''The four year separation was hard for me. I wasn't divorced, but I wasn't married either. I lived in limbo. I tried dating, but I felt too guilty, like I was cheating. So I focused on getting through college. I'd always wanted to be a teacher. I worked to pay the bills and spent all my free time studying. Sometimes—''

She could feel herself blushing again. She forced herself to continue. ''Sometimes I got so lonely, I let Tom come back for a couple of days. I knew it was wrong, that it would only drag out the divorce, but...'' Her voice trailed off. ''That's what happened four months ago. Afterward I was so angry with myself that I finally agreed to let my lawyer file papers forcing Tom to sign the divorce decree. The next day he was killed.''

She closed her eyes against the memories, then opened them and stared at Shane. She still wasn't sure what he was thinking, but his gaze never wavered from hers.

''I hated myself for my weakness,'' she said. ''Then about three weeks after his death, I realized I was pregnant. In that moment, I felt God was telling me that it was okay. That Tom had finally done something right. I've always wanted lots of children and I'd begun to think that wasn't going to happen. So while I regret a lot of things in my life, I could never regret my baby.''

Shane raised his hand, then stopped. His expression tightened. Low in her stomach, tension formed, but not the good kind. He was judging her and finding her wanting.

''What are you thinking?'' she asked, because she had to know, even if it was bad.

''That you're the most amazing woman I've ever met.''

She blinked. ''What?''

This time when he raised his hand, he cupped her cheek. ''You've been through hell and back and you completed the journey with grace and strength. And you are so incredibly beautiful.''

Her mouth opened, but she couldn't speak. Beautiful? Her? She was bruised and mussed and pregnant and—

He swore under his breath and straightened. ''Sorry. That last part wasn't supposed to come out.

The last thing you need in your life is some guy coming on to you. I apologize.''

Coming on to her? As in, he found her attractive in *that way?*

"Shane?"

"Pretty stupid of me, huh?" He wasn't looking at her anymore. "Look, it's late. I should let you get some sleep." He started to stand up.

She put her hand on his arm to stop him. "Don't apologize. Please. I like that you think I'm attractive." She couldn't bring herself to say beautiful. "If it makes you feel any better, I think the same of you. That you're handsome and strong and dependable and..."

Was it her imagination or had he just moved closer? "And what?" he asked.

"Sexy," she whispered.

He groaned low in his throat. "Angela, I want—"

"Me, too."

And then he kissed her.

Chapter Five

Shane's mouth was firm and warm against hers. Angela melted into him, wondering how it was possible to have known him for such a short time yet want so desperately to be in his arms. One of his hands rubbed against her back while the other cradled her head. His lips pressed, then teased as he kissed her.

The night seemed to surround them in a cocoon of safe, silent darkness. Shane shifted so he was closer and she wrapped her arms around him, holding on and wanting never to let go.

The kiss lingered. Angela sensed it was up to her—that he would read her signals and do as much or as little as she let him. Perhaps it would be wise to break the kiss now, to leave it polite and innocent. But she didn't want to. The passion that she'd flirted with before returned again, only a hundred times stronger. She found herself wanting to *be* with this man with a desire she'd never experienced before. In high school she'd kissed one or two boys, but nothing had come of the relationships. Tom was the only man to have known her intimately. Still, despite her lack of experience, she sensed that something incredible had happened between herself and Shane.

When he angled his head slightly so he could deepen the kiss, she found herself catching her breath. When his tongue lightly traced her lower lip, she parted for him, desperate to have him inside her mouth. She wanted to know him and taste him, to learn his textures, his heat, to feel his body, his hands, his very maleness, all of him.

His tongue brushed against hers. Instantly fire exploded inside of her. She couldn't breathe or think—she could only feel. Feel and need with a strength that left her shaken to the core of her being. If he'd pushed her on her back and started making love with her right there, she could not have refused him. All her life she'd read stories about passion and love. She'd wondered what it was those couples felt for each other, and for the first time, she understood. Understood and reveled in the differences between a man and a woman. She was soft to his hard, yielding to his readiness, aching for him.

She traced her hand up his back and slid her fingers through his short hair. One of his hands dropped to her thigh while the other cupped her jaw, then her cheek. He breathed her name in a voice thick with passion and desire. She could feel herself swelling and dampening for him. Her breasts ached. She desperately wanted him to touch her there.

Then, as if he read her mind, the hand on her thigh lifted slowly and brushed against one erect nipple. She gasped, then plunged her tongue into his mouth. He accepted her passion and returned it with his own. As they danced together, imitating the most intimate dance of all, he stroked her full curves, discovering her shape, her sensitivity, making her moan and softly beg.

She was lost in a sensual fog and she never wanted to find her way home. This was what it was supposed to be, she realized, half stunned, half empowered by the realization that her body had potential she'd never known.

He brought both of his hands up to her face and held her still, then pulled back enough to kiss her nose, her cheeks, her chin, then gave one last brush against her mouth.

"Shane," she whispered, and slowly opened her eyes.

He stared at her, looking as stunned and aroused she felt. The single bedside lamp did little to chase away shadows and in the darkness, his brown eyes looked black and bottomless.

"Wow," he breathed.

"Yeah. That was unexpected."

"For me, too." He smiled at her. His gaze traced her face, then dropped lower. Instantly his expression changed. The passion fled, replaced by regret and horror. "What the hell was I thinking?" he growled and stood. He swore again. "I'm sorry, Angela. That was incredibly pushy and insensitive. You're my guest and under my protection, you're also…" He waved vaguely toward her midsection.

Her mind cleared slowly. Desire made it hard to think, although his initial look of dismay had cleared away most of the cobwebs.

"Are you apologizing because I'm pregnant, or because you're sorry?"

He stared at her. "Because you're pregnant. I should never have done that. It's wrong." He shoved a hand through his slightly mussed hair.

Angela remained on the bed. From her sitting position, she couldn't help noticing the rather large bulge at the front of his jeans. At least he'd enjoyed their encounter as much as she had, even if he was having second thoughts.

Shane sucked in a breath. "I don't know what got into me. One minute you were talking and the next I just wanted to kiss you."

He hesitated and she had a brief flash of insight that kissing wasn't all he'd wanted to do. He'd wanted to make love with her.

She smiled at him. "Stop apologizing."

"But I—"

"No. Listen to me. I'm beat-up, bruised and pregnant. I just found out that a good-looking, single guy finds me attractive enough to want to kiss me." *And do other things.* But she didn't mention that. It was enough to have the information to hold

close to her heart. "I'm flattered. I'm thrilled. And
I was caught up in the kiss as much as you were."
Maybe more.

He frowned. "You're not mad?"

"No."

His mouth curved up slightly. "So it's okay?"

"It's more than okay. Feel free to distract me
from my nightmares with kisses anytime." She
wanted to say more. She wanted to talk about what
she'd felt when they were holding each other, but
she was afraid. Everything had happened so fast
and what if he hadn't felt it as well?

"Okay. If you're sure." He shoved his hands
into his jeans, then seemed to realize they were unfastened. He glanced down and saw how his arousal
showed. Faint color darkened his cheeks. "Well,
it's late. I should let you get some sleep."

She would rather he'd returned to her bed, but
he wasn't offering that as one of the options. So
she simply nodded and wished him a good night.
When he was gone and the lights were out, she
thought about how he'd made her feel when he
kissed her. There was passion between them, but
there was something else, as well. Something like
respect. After years of living with a man who
dreamed rather than did, she understood the value
of planning and follow through. She'd learned to
look at a man's character as well as his easy smile
and his words. In Shane she'd found someone who
had started with nothing and had made a world for
himself. Her feelings about him were easy to understand, but what did he think about her?

* * *

Angela checked on the pot roast in the oven. She was slow-cooking the large piece of meat at a low temperature. Normally she would have used an electric frying pan, but Shane didn't seem to possess one. As she straightened, she caught sight of the clock just above the burners. According to Shane's quick call less than an hour ago, he should be home any minute.

Despite the fact that it had been three days…or nights…since they'd kissed and not once had it been repeated, her heart still sped up in anticipation of her seeing him. She would have thought that familiarity would have eased her attraction, but it was the just opposite. The more time she spent with him, the more time she *wanted* to spend with him. She'd never felt this kind of intense longing before—not even when she'd first met Tom.

Maybe it was because she and Shane got along so well. That first morning after their kiss could have been awkward. She'd been more than a little nervous as she'd made her way to the kitchen. But instead of acting as if nothing had happened, Shane had instantly confessed that he'd been awake all night, thinking about what had happened, or not happened, between them. She'd admitted to the same affliction. They'd both laughed and had mutually agreed they could have been an alternative energy source for the town that night.

Somehow bringing their attraction out into the open had defused a little of the tension. She found it easy to fall into a routine in Shane's house. Most of the time she was able to forget that she was under a loose form of protective custody and that until the kidnappers were caught, she was at risk.

Angela moved to the cookies cooling on the counter. She'd made a batch of peanut butter a couple of days ago, and chocolate chips ones earlier that afternoon. Shane had admitted to a weakness for home-baked goodies and she couldn't help indulging him. One of the things she'd missed most when her marriage had ended was the simple pleasure she found in cooking. Dishes for one hadn't seemed that exciting. Besides, in the past month or so, her taste for sweets had increased.

She pressed her hand to her stomach and smiled. Whatever else Tom had done wrong with his life, at the end, he'd done the most right thing of all. She was having a baby and nothing else mattered.

Since arriving at Shane's house, she'd started making peace with her past. She knew that as her daughter grew up, she was going to tell her all about her father. Tom would never be more than a memory to his child, but she was determined to make it a good one.

The sound of footsteps on the back porch distracted her. Happily she moved toward the rear of the kitchen just as Shane walked in through the utility room. He was handsome as always in his khaki uniform. At the sight of her, his strong face broke into a smile.

"How was your day?" he asked.

"Great. And yours?" Without thinking, she kept moving toward him until she was close enough to place her hands on his shoulders. She raised herself up on her toes to kiss him, but something in his manner alerted her. Instead of responding, he stiffened for a split second before meeting her halfway. His mouth brushed against her cheek.

At that moment Angela realized she'd been so caught up in thinking about Tom and Shane and how at home she felt here, that she'd reacted without thinking. She wasn't Shane's wife, greeting him after a long day. She was a friend, or at the very least, a civilian in trouble.

She lowered herself to her heels and took a step away from him. She could feel the heat on her cheeks. "Sorry," she said quickly. "I wasn't thinking. I didn't mean to…" Her voice trailed off.

Shane saved her. He leaned forward and touched the tip of her nose. "No, problem, Angela. I'm happy to see you, too."

Angela shifted uncomfortably. Could she have been more stupid? She sighed. Probably not. It was distressing.

"We have some news on the kidnapping," he said. "It's not much, but it's a start. The kidnappers have asked for a million dollar ransom. The good news is they've been in touch with authorities, and we know the little girl is safe."

"Thank God for that," Angela said sincerely. "I think about that poor child a lot. If only she hadn't been there at that moment in time. It's so horrible and unfair."

"Hey. It's not your fault. Remember?"

"I know. I've been thinking about what happened that day. I know I'm not responsible. I just wish there was something I could have done to help. As an adult, I would be better equipped to handle a kidnapping.''

''I don't think anyone deals with that well. What happened is done. Now we have to concentrate on keeping you safe and rescuing the child. The rest of it will take care of itself.''

She nodded. He was right. ''Thanks for being so understanding.''

''No problem''

He took a deep breath. ''Something smells great. Let me go get changed into jeans and then you can tell me all about dinner.''

He left the room before she could ask if it was okay for her to watch him undress. Angela sighed. ''For a pregnant woman, you seem to have a one-track mind,'' she murmured to herself.

She didn't remember ever thinking about sex as much as she had in the past three days. She'd even read through a couple of the prenatal books she'd brought with her from Houston. In them the authors had assured the reader that making love was perfectly safe unless the couple had been told otherwise by a doctor. Angela knew she was about as healthy as she could be, so maybe her urges weren't so unnatural, after all. The problem was, she seemed to be the only one having them. As far as she could tell, Shane wasn't even thinking about their kiss anymore, let alone wishing they would do it again. Maybe his long sleepless night had gotten it out of his system.

She took a seat in the kitchen to wait for him to return. She knew exactly what was going to happen then, too. She would take one look at him in worn jeans and a long-sleeved flannel shirt and her heart rate would climb to triple digits. It had happened every evening so far, so there was no reason for her to think it would change. The worst of it was, she hated flannel shirts. So why did Shane's look so good on him?

About two minutes later he walked back into the kitchen. As she'd predicted, her heart kicked into overdrive and her breathing increased. At least she was sitting so she didn't have to worry about her knees giving way.

"You don't have to do this," he said.

It took her a moment to realize he was holding a pile of clean laundry in his hands. Laundry that she'd left on his bed. He wasn't talking about her overreaction to his flannel shirt.

"You're here because I invited you," he told her. "Not to be my housekeeper."

Angela smiled at him. It was the same friendly, open smile she always gave him, and as usual, it hit him low in the gut. Shane stifled a groan.

"I have to do something to fill my day," she said. "I've never been much for daytime television, so the hours can get pretty long. Beside, a couple of loads of laundry hardly equal your hospitality."

"You're cooking, too," he reminded her.

She was taking care of him. That's really what had him rattled, he admitted to himself. No one had done that before. While they'd been dating, Mary had gone out of her way to prove that she was an independent woman, and not any man's slave. They'd never lived together, so there had been no sharing of domestic duties. While he'd been in foster care, most of the mothers had worked at least part-time. He'd been expected to take care of himself and do things such as his own laundry.

"All right, you caught me," Angela said with a laugh. "I'm paying for my keep with services. Is that so bad?"

He couldn't answer. Mostly because he had a vision of a different kind of service...one they could perform on each other. An intimate kind of—*Don't go there,* he warned himself. It was ten kinds of trouble.

He set the laundry on the far kitchen chair, then pulled out the one next to her and sat. "I guess not. But don't overtire yourself. You have to think about the baby."

"I do. Constantly. Look at it this way, Shane. Right after the holiday break in January, I'm going to be teaching full-time. Compared to that, doing a little laundry is nothing."

He leaned toward her. "You'll be teaching? You heard from the principal?"

She nodded enthusiastically. Her short hair danced across her forehead. Wide green eyes sparkled with excitement. "She called me today. She told me that she still wanted me for the job. I start the second week of January and work for as long as I can. Then I go back in September." She pressed her hands together. "It's perfect. I'm so thrilled."

"So you'll be staying in Whitehorn permanently." The thought pleased him. He hadn't wanted to think about Angela moving on.

"Once this other business is settled, I'll find a place of my own. I know I've been cutting into your wild bachelor life-style."

"Oh, sure. Normally I'm out every night."

Her humor faded. "You should be, Shane. I still don't understand why you've cut yourself off for so long. And don't bother giving me all that nonsense about not being the kind of man who commits or who's a good father. Men who are commitment phobic don't buy houses like this one."

She had a point, but he wasn't quite willing to admit that. "Why Whitehorn?" he asked to shift the focus away from himself. "You could have moved anywhere."

"I know. I wanted a small town where I could belong. That's been my goal since my mom died—to find a home of my own. I randomly picked three different towns in three different states, then sent away for information. Based on what I received back, I like Whitehorn the best."

She glanced around the kitchen. "Just look at this place. It's bright and cheerful, very homey. It's exactly the kind of house I've always wanted. From the little I've seen of Whitehorn, I could easily find another house like this."

He stared at her. She'd stopped wearing a bandage, so the stitches on her temple were clearly visible. The bruises had turned bright purple. But none of that mattered. What he saw was a beautiful woman with a good heart. If she hadn't been, she wouldn't have stayed to take care of her brothers and sisters, putting her own dreams on hold. She was smart and nurturing, a born teacher...or mother.

''You have an odd expression on your face. What are you thinking?'' she asked.

''That Mary never liked this house. She wanted something bigger.''

Angela's gaze met his. ''Mary was stupid about a lot of things.''

For the first time Shane wondered if Angela was right.

Chapter Six

Less than twenty minutes after Shane left on his "boys' night out" with five-year-old J.J., there was a knock on the front door. Angela had her hand on the dead bolt when she remembered his instructions about not letting anyone in unless she knew them or they could produce identification showing they were with the sheriff's department. In the nearly two weeks she'd lived with him, no one had come calling.

"Who is it?" she asked.

"Nancy," a woman answered. "Your neighbor."

Angela didn't know whether to laugh or groan. She didn't need anything to jog her memory. Who could forget the fabulously attractive, leggy brunette who lived next door? She'd seen her outside watering her yard or playing with her children several times over the past week and a half. Even in her scruffiest clothing, she looked like a model on a photo shoot. It was very discouraging.

Angela opened the door. Nancy smiled at her and held out a plate of perfectly iced sugar cookies. "Hi. I've been meaning to come by and get to know you, but I wasn't sure how you were feeling. In my opinion, sugar of any kind heals most female woes."

"I agree," Angela said, then wondered if Nancy actually ever ate food. Or maybe she was one of those disgusting people who stayed thin regardless of what she consumed. "Come on in. Shane just left, but as he took your son with him, you already know that."

Nancy walked into the house with the ease of someone who had been a guest many times in the past. "Isn't it great?" she said as she led the way to the kitchen. "He and J.J. have always been close. Belinda is spending the night with my mom and Jerry, my husband, is working late, so I thought I'd take a chance that you'd like a little company." She paused in the middle of the kitchen. "I should confess that I have an ulterior motive for being here, though." Her smile broadened. "I plan to pump you shamelessly for gossip about your relationship with Shane."

"Pump away," Angela said, motioning to the table by the large window. "There's not much to tell."

She walked to the counter and poured Nancy coffee from the pot, then got herself a glass of milk. As she crossed the floor to take a seat opposite her guest, she tried not to notice how Nancy's shoulder-length curls caught the light, or her perfect face with its big eyes and pouty mouth. She was definitely not going to acknowledge the other woman's incredible figure. Angela suddenly felt as if the slight rounding of her stomach had grown until her belly was the size of a watermelon. Then she sighed. It wasn't Nancy's fault she was so physically amazing.

Nancy leaned forward and rested one perfectly manicured hand on the table. "I didn't even know Shane was dating anyone, let alone to the point of having you move in." Her gaze dropped to Angela's stomach, but she didn't say anything about the pregnancy. "I thought we were close enough to talk about most things, but I guess I was wrong. At first I was really hurt by that, but then I decided that the most important thing was Shane's happiness. After what happened with his fiancée, he shut himself away for a year, then he dated for a while. But recently he's been Mr. Reclusive. I'm just glad he's found someone to care about him."

Angela stared at her. What was she supposed to say? "I thought Shane had told you why I was here."

Nancy frowned. "He said you were a friend who had been attacked by those men who kidnapped that poor little girl. He was keeping you here until you'd recovered." She motioned to Angela's still fading bruises. "Those look a lot better than they did when you arrived."

"I feel better," Angela said slowly. "Everything Shane told you about his relationship with me is true. So why would you think that we're involved?"

Nancy grabbed a cookie and took a bite. "Because there's no other reason he would invite someone to live in his house. Shane isn't the most social guy on the planet. I'm not saying he's weird or anything, but he's a typical male who kind of keeps to himself. He resists getting involved until it feels right. From what he's told me, he went so slow with Mary that he almost lost her. I remember him mentioning they had nearly a month of dating before he even kissed her good-night. Shane is many wonderful things, but he's not impulsive when it comes to women."

Angela did her best to keep her face impassive. Was Nancy telling the truth? But why would Shane's friend lie? Still, her description of Shane was nothing like the man Angela knew. Shane *was* impulsive—the fact that he'd invited her to stay here, not to mention their kiss last week, proved that.

"So, tell me everything," Nancy said. "Start with your first date and spill as many details as you're comfortable with. Although I have to warn you, I'm going to ask tons of questions." She finished her cookie. "I still can't believe that man kept me in the dark about this." She shook her head. "Would you like to go to dinner with my husband

and me? Maybe we can pick a night next week. I have several great sitters right here in the neighborhood, so leaving the kids isn't a problem. In fact sometime I think those little munchkins are thrilled when we leave them behind. I know they get spoiled rotten, regardless of who stays with them.''

Angela stared at her, then blinked. ''I don't know what question to answer first.''

Nancy laughed. ''I know. I talk too much. Jerry tells me that all the time. Just tell me about you and Shane and I'll be quiet.''

Angela felt a sharp pain in her chest. At first she wasn't sure what it was, then she realized it was longing. She wanted to tell Nancy that she and Shane were a couple. She wanted to share girl-talk about how they'd met and their first date. She wanted to confess details about their planned future. Because even though she'd only known him for a short time, she'd already come to see that he was everything she'd ever wanted in a man. Except he wasn't really interested in her.

Oh, sure, he'd kissed her, but that didn't mean anything significant. It had been a reaction to the moment, and apparently something he hadn't had any trouble not doing again. It had been almost a week and there hadn't been a single repeat of the kiss. The morning after, when he'd confessed his attraction, she'd allowed herself to hope there might be a chance of something between them. But since then she'd decided that he must have just been being kind.

''There's nothing to tell,'' Angela said quietly.

"Shane and I aren't an item." She recounted the story of her attack and how she'd awakened to find Shane in her hospital room. "When it was time for me to leave the hospital, he brought me here so I would be safe."

Nancy's gaze settled on her stomach. "So the baby isn't his."

"No. I'm a widow. My husband and I had separated for some time before his death. There was a brief reconciliation—" She pressed her lips together. "No, that's wrong. I'm trying to make it prettier than it was. He came by one night and I was lonely. I let him stay."

Nancy picked up her mug of coffee and held it in both hands. "I understand completely. Jerry and I bought our house shortly after we were married. Shane moved in a couple of years later. He was engaged to Mary and excited about getting married and starting a family. Then she left and he was pretty destroyed. Six months later, I had my first baby."

She looked at Angela and shrugged. "Jerry and I were both young. We didn't handle the stress very well. When J.J. was about six months old, Jerry and I separated for a time. He moved out. The days were really long without him and I was lonely. I'd gained a lot of weight, I thought I was an ugly cow, and here was this attractive, single guy living next door."

Angela sensed what she was going to say, even before she said it. The pain in her chest sharpened.

Jealousy, she thought, which was crazy. She didn't know Shane well enough to be jealous, yet she was.

"One night, after fortifying myself with wine, I came over here and tried to seduce Shane," Nancy said softly. "He was very sweet, but very firm. He said to get my butt back to my house and try to fix things with my husband. I found out later that he'd called Jerry after I left and read him the riot act. Basically Shane told him he was a fool to lose the best wife and kid any man ever had and if he didn't fix things with me, then Shane was going to give my phone number to all his single friends."

Her pain eased a little and Angela was able to nod and even smile. "He was a good friend to you both."

"The best," Nancy said. "Jerry and I started talking. We went into counseling and within two months, he'd moved back. Our marriage is stronger than ever, and all because of Shane. So you can see that we both owe him. I've been waiting and waiting for the right woman to come along."

Maybe it was the fact that she hadn't talked to any of her friends in Houston for a long time, or maybe it was that Nancy had just shared something very personal. For whatever reason, Angela found herself wanting to tell this woman the truth.

"If you're trying to hint that Shane is one of the good guys," Angela said, "I already know that. To be honest, he's about the best man I've ever met. But he's not going to be interested in me."

"Whyever not?"

Angela laughed, but the sound was faintly strangled. "Look at me. I'm pregnant with another man's child. It's possible that my late husband might have been involved with something illegal, I don't know. I've barely arrived in Whitehorn, so I don't have any friends or family here. I have very little to offer someone like Shane."

Nancy leaned close and covered Angela's hand with her own. "First of all, you do have friends. I consider myself one and I hope you feel the same. Second, you're not still mourning your husband and you're not responsible for his mistakes. Shane is going to understand that. Finally, Shane is the kind of man to care more about a woman's future than her past. From what I can see, he's already bent his own particular rules and let you into his life. Don't discount that. And don't let fear keep you from reaching out for someone very special."

"You don't know how much I want what you're saying to be true."

"So believe me." Nancy squeezed her hand, then released her. "Oh, and you might try seducing him. It didn't work for me, but I have a feeling that you'll do much better in that department."

Angela grimaced. "Yeah, right. Look at us. If he didn't want you, what makes you think he'll want me?"

Nancy's expression turned knowing. "I've seen the look on his face when he talks about you. The man has it bad."

Hope took the place of the pain in her chest—a hope that burned as bright as a shooting star. With Tom she thought she'd found what she'd been looking for, but she'd been wrong. Was she going to get a second chance at love? Did Shane really think she was attractive and was he willing to overlook the fact that she carried another man's child?

"If you don't ask, you'll never know," Nancy told her.

"I had the *best* time, Uncle Shane," J.J. said as he gave Shane a hug.

"Me, too, kid." Shane set the boy on the ground and winked at Nancy. "I only let him have one beer tonight and we kept the cussing to a minimum."

J.J. giggled, then waved his new toy truck in the air. "I wanna show Daddy what Uncle Shane won for me."

Nancy pointed to the rear of the house. "He's watching the basketball game in the family room, but don't get too involved, J.J. It's a school night and you have to be in bed in fifteen minutes."

"Basketball!" J.J. yelled as he ran out of the room.

Nancy motioned for Shane to take a seat in the living room, but he shook his head. "I've got to get home. I just wanted to tell you that everything went great."

"It always does." She studied his face. "It's time to stop pretending, young man. Quit being a part-time father to my kids and go make some of your own."

Shane stiffened. Although they'd had this same conversation on and off for the past four years, this time things were different. This time he'd begun to hope it might be possible.

He knew it was crazy. He knew that he and Angela didn't know enough about each other, yet nothing had ever felt so right. But he'd thought that about Mary and he'd been wrong. Eight years in different foster homes had taught him how hard things could get.

"Gee, you're being quiet," Nancy said. "Normally you politely tell me to mind my own business. Something must be different."

"I don't know. Maybe." He wanted things to be different, but he wasn't sure.

"I talked with her tonight while you were gone," she said.

"What?"

"I know, it's incredibly nosy of me, but I couldn't help myself. I went over, armed with cookies, and had a nice talk with Angela. I like her very much, despite the fact that she told me you two were only friends. You had me going there, Shane. I thought the baby was yours."

"It's not and we *are* just friends. She needed a place to stay and I offered mine." At least, that was how it had started.

"Interesting. And this from a man who values privacy above most things."

"I know, but this is different."

"Why?"

A reasonable question from a close friend, but one for which he had no answer. "I wish I knew."

"From what I could pry out of her, you're both

single, you're both intelligent and you're both attracted to each other.''

That got his attention. He stared at her. "She said she was attracted to me?"

"No, and even if she had, I wouldn't tell you. It's a girl thing. I'm basing that statement on what I've observed about both of you. You both glow when you talk about the other person.''

He could feel himself glowing right now. Angela wanted him? He'd known that she'd liked their kiss nearly as much as he had, but with all that was going on in her life, he hadn't wanted to push her too far, too fast.

"How do you feel about her baby?" Nancy asked. "You're not the father."

"I know, and it doesn't bother me." He told her about seeing the photo from the sonogram. "It was the most amazing thing—to look at a simple picture and know that very same child was growing inside of her."

Nancy gave him a quick smile. "I think the two of you are going to do just fine. Just don't wait too long to say something, Shane. I think it would be very sad if the two of you missed out on each other because you were both so busy giving each other plenty of time."

She had a point, but he also had to be careful. "I'll keep that in mind." He bent and kissed her cheek. "Tell Jerry that he's a lucky guy."

"I share that piece of information with him every night."

Shane waved goodbye and let himself out the

front door. Usually after he and J.J. spent time together, he stayed to talk with Jerry and Nancy, but tonight he wanted to get home. As he crossed the driveway and walked up to his front door, he saw a light glowing from inside. That's what happened now that Angela was in his life—she kept a light on for him. It was small gesture, but one that pleased and touched him.

He used his key to unlock the front door, then stepped inside. "It's me," he called.

"Thank goodness." Angela walked in from the kitchen and laughed. "I've been alone with a plate of cookies for far too long. I keep telling myself to freeze them, but one by one they're disappearing inside of me. For some reason I can resist my own baking, but someone else's is usually beyond tempting and I give in. How was your evening with J.J.?"

She was casually dressed in leggings and a dark red long-sleeved sweatshirt. Gold heart-shaped earrings caught the light and twinkled. Her mouth curved up in its usual welcoming smile. In that moment he knew that he wanted to pull her close and hold her. He wanted to kiss her and touch her and make love with her. He wanted his feelings to be real. What he wanted was a sure thing. But life wasn't usually that accommodating.

"We had a great time. Pizza and video games. It was a guy's paradise."

"Ah, I see. So for a change of pace, you'll be happy to watch a period movie with me on public television, right? It starts in about fifteen minutes.

Of course there's also a basketball game on. What a dilemma.''

Her green eyes danced with amusement. No matter what the circumstances, she brightened his day. He suspected her good nature was a testament to her strength of character. She'd gone through far more than most people, and yet she'd kept her sense of humor. She was the kind of person who would always survive with dignity and courage intact. '

He wanted her—of that he was sure. But for the rest of it...he still had questions. His past had taught him to be wary. Yet when he looked at her all he could think about was being with her.

"Who are you?" he asked, his voice low and gravelly. "Who is this woman who has invaded my life, my thoughts and my world? I can't stop thinking about you...wanting you. Am I crazy? Is that wrong?"

Her gaze never wavered from his. He'd thought she might retreat or act nervous. She did blush a little, but she also took a step toward him and stood tall. "If you're crazy, then I am, too, because I feel exactly the same."

Chapter Seven

This wasn't happening, Angela thought with a combination of joy, trepidation, and, embarrassingly enough, lust. It couldn't be. Had Shane really just admitted that he couldn't stop thinking about her? Had she really invaded his world as much as he'd invaded hers? She pressed her hands together, wanting to believe it was all true, but part of her was afraid. To be so close to something she wanted, and then to lose it—she knew she would survive, but it wouldn't be pretty.

It was probably just hormones and a lack of sex, but was that so bad? She liked Shane. She really did. Maybe more than liked, but she would worry about that later. However, before they could act on any mutual desire, she had to ask him how he felt—

about Tom and about the baby. No matter what that truth cost her.

"Shane, there's something I have to talk to you about," she said softly, not quite able to meet his gaze.

"All right. Talk to me."

She took in a deep breath. "One of the reasons I fell in love with Tom was the way he treated me. From the moment he met me, he thought I was special."

"I remember. He thought you were a princess."

She nodded. "I had been taking care of my brothers and sisters for so long, and before them I'd been looking after my mom before she passed away. I couldn't remember the last time anything had been about me. Tom changed all that and for a while it was wonderful. But it wasn't what I needed."

She risked a glance at him. He was watching her intently, but she didn't see any judgment in his expression. "Go on," he told her.

"It took me a long time, but I finally saw that instead of picking a man who would be there for me through my future, I picked someone to make up for my past. Between that mistake on my part and Tom's inability to grow up, I suspect we were destined to failure."

"You can't blame yourself for that," Shane said. "You had no way of knowing what you were doing at the time."

"I know. I've learned that over the years. I made the best decision I could at the time. And that's my point. I can't regret marrying Tom, because he gave me my child. I can't regret the baby. I keeping wondering if this new life is going to be the best thing he ever did.''

Shane moved toward her and gently touched her cheek. ''You don't have to explain this to me. I understand completely. One of the things I like most about you is your ability to forgive Tom his weaknesses and to focus on the good in the man. You're even working on forgiving yourself. That's what matters. That and the fact that you'll love your child, regardless of how she came to be.''

Her eyes burned with unshed tears. ''Thank you,'' she whispered.

''Don't thank me. If I didn't think that, I wouldn't be worth bothering with.''

He continued to stroke her face. The touch was light and gentle, and very, very sensual.

''I remember being happy when I was young,'' he said. ''Before my parents died, I mean. Most of the memories are pretty blurry, but what I can see is a lot of laughter. They were very much in love and I was the bright spot in their universe. I always wanted that same joy when I had a family of my own. But I was always afraid.''

''Why?'' she asked, searching his gaze. ''I've told you a dozen times, you're a natural father. You'll be great with kids.''

''It's not that,'' he admitted. ''It's not what I had, it's what I lost. When my parents were killed, I was devastated. I'd lost everything, and I was only nine. Life got ugly really fast.''

"I'm sorry," she told him as she pressed her cheek into his hand. The warmth of his touch connected them, she thought. She wanted to move closer and hold him, but sensed he had to finish what he was telling her first.

"After that I got cautious," he said. "I didn't want to lose anyone again, so I didn't get too close. That way there was nothing to take away. I thought if I planned everything, if I made sure I had backup plans and contingencies, then I would never be caught off guard again."

Of course, she thought. It made perfect sense. "What happened instead is that you spent most of your time alone. Until Mary, and then she let you down, too."

"I want to believe," he admitted. "I want to care, maybe even love…"

But he didn't. Angela told herself she understood. "Everything has happened so fast," she murmured.

His fingers continued to stroke her cheek. "I need you, Angela. It's been a long time since I've needed anyone."

Need was a start, she thought. After all she wasn't a hundred percent sure either. She stared at the handsome face which had become so dear and so familiar. Okay, she was ninety-eight percent sure, but he didn't have to know that. They could be lovers for a while and see where that went. After all Nancy had said Shane was already acting out of character. It was a hopeful sign.

"I need you, too," she admitted.

Shane dropped his hands to his sides and shifted

uncomfortably. "At the risk of being a clod, how are you defining 'need?'"

She smiled. She knew exactly what he meant. "Oh, I was thinking naked and in bed. What about you?"

His groan was audible. "Thank goodness. I want you so much. I have from the beginning. Not just from the kiss but from the first time I saw you."

His words thrilled her. "Really?"

"Yeah."

He reached for her, then paused. "What about the baby? I don't want to hurt either of you."

Angela threw herself at him, wrapping her arms around his waist and resting her head on his chest. "Thank you," she murmured. "Thank you for being so warm and caring. This is one of the reasons I feel so safe with you." She raised her head and stared at his handsome face. "I'm perfectly healthy and the baby is going to be just fine. It's possible that in the last few weeks of pregnancy things will change, but for now, it's perfectly safe."

"So you're saying we shouldn't waste any time."

She laughed. "Something like that."

He cupped her face, then lowered his head and kissed her. The touch of his mouth against hers was welcome and familiar. He was as she remembered—the feel of his lips, his scent, his heat. And her body responded to his closeness and his touch. She felt a warmth start low in her belly and flow into her most feminine place. She felt her breasts swell and pucker. Even as she brought her arms up and wrapped them around his neck, she marveled in the rightness of the moment. She and Shane had only kissed once before. Yet being with him this way was a homecoming.

"I want you," he breathed against her mouth, then slipped his tongue past her parted lips and invaded her.

In that moment Angela found herself caught up in a wild, tumultuous storm. She felt buffed from all sides as incredible waves of passion crashed through. As he stroked against the inside of her lower lip, then teased her tongue with his, she found herself unable to do anything but cling to his broad shoulders and drown in the pleasure he created.

It was just a kiss, but it was also the portal into a new world. She ran her hands up and down his back, reveling in the muscles that clenched and bunched as she touched them, sensing he wanted her to learn him as he would learn her. They had chosen each other, perhaps for the night...perhaps longer. Regardless, she still needed to know everything about him.

His tongue plunged inside her mouth again and again, leaving her breathless and shaking. Then he cupped her face and rained kisses on her cheeks, her forehead, her closed eyes, before nibbling his way from her jaw to the collar of her sweatshirt.

"I want you," he breathed between kisses. "I need you, Angela. Let me touch you and be inside you." He raised his head and stared into her eyes. "Please."

She had never felt such absolute power—and

such incredible humility. They were united souls, broken apart and left to wander unfulfilled until they found each other again.

"I need you, too," she told him. "I need to be yours, in every sense of the word."

With that he took her hand and led her down the narrow hallway and into his bedroom. Once there he turned on the overhead light.

She had a brief impression of a large four-poster bed and an oversize dresser. No rugs broke the stretch of hardwood floor, no pictures relieved the stark white of the walls. The comforter was beige, and there wasn't a throw pillow in sight.

"You aren't much for decorating, are you?" she teased. "Would it kill you to put up a poster or two? Just something for color."

"I never saw the point," he told her. "I did this room myself. Mary never stayed here with me. We never made love in this house or in this bed. I want you to know that because I don't want there to be any ghosts."

She faced him and put her hands on his waist. "If you can understand and let go of my past, then I can certainly do the same."

"I'm glad."

He reached for the hem of her sweatshirt and pulled it up. Angela hesitated for a split second. Although she was barely showing, her body was still different from the way it had been before she'd gotten pregnant. Would Shane want her once he'd seen her naked?

But he was tugging on her shirt and unless she

wanted to explain about her personal insecurities, she couldn't stop him now. Besides, she doubted that he would understand. Most guys never quite got the whole female - body - image - fear - thing women carried around in their heads.

She raised her arms and let him pull the sweat-shirt over her head. He tossed it onto the dresser.

Next he knelt in front of her and carefully un-fastened her shoes and took them off, along with her socks. He pulled down her leggings, easing them off each foot. She stood in front of him in panties and her bra and it was all she could not to dive under the covers and pull a blanket up to her neck. A picture of his neighbor flashed into her brain. No doubt Nancy had been radiant from the day she'd been born. At least Shane hadn't had an intimate relationship with her, so he wouldn't be comparing the two of them.

"What are you thinking?" he asked.

"Nothing." She pressed her lips together. She'd never been a very good liar and Shane didn't look the least bit convinced. She sighed. "Just that I'm a little self-conscious about my body. I mean, it's okay most of the time, but I'm pregnant now and I'm, you know, worried you won't like it."

Her voice had lowered as she'd spoken until the last few words came out as a whisper. She also found herself staring intently at the top button of Shane's shirt. It was really a fascinating item, she told herself as she tried to avoid his gaze.

"How can you doubt that you're beautiful?" he asked, then took her hand in his and pressed it against his groin. "How can you doubt that I want you?"

The thick length of his arousal surged against her palm. He was certainly...ready. A smile tugged at the corner of her mouth. "So how long has it been, Deputy?"

"A lifetime," he said, picking her up into his arms and lowering her onto the mattress. "I've been waiting for you since before I was born."

As lines went, it was a darn good one, she thought dreamily as he claimed her mouth with his. She liked how he pressed against her, too, his body hard to her soft. He was all unyielding planes and masculine strength. One of his large hands splayed across her body, between the gentle rise of her belly and the bottom of her bra. As his tongue swept the inside of her mouth, she vaguely wondered which direction he would move first. There were so many possibilities with each.

Then, slowly, so very slowly that she thought she would die, he moved his fingers up until he cupped the curve of her left breast. He brushed the underside, teasing her until her nipple was as hard as a pebble and literally aching with need. He angled his head and kissed her deeper, but it wasn't enough. She wanted him to touch her bare breast, to stroke the sensitive tip, to rub it and squeeze it, to lick it with his tongue and drive her mad.

As least he could read her mind, she thought as he reached underneath her and searched for the fastening on her bra. When he found it, he undid the hooks one by one. Then he slid the undergarment down her arms and tossed it away.

The night air was cool on her overheated skin. Her nipples puckered even more, making them hypersensitive. His hand returned to cup her curves, then his thumb brushed against the ready peak.

A million dots of light burst free inside of her. Angela surged against him, pulling his tongue deeper as they kissed, sucking on him, all the while willing him to keep touching her that way. He continued to read her mind. He stroked her over and over again, taking her nipple between his thumb and forefinger and teasing it until she thought she would die or climax. If he'd even lightly brushed against her feminine place while he was doing that, she would have lost herself in release. She could feel the tightness in her body, the need coiling low. Her skin had never been this sensitive, her body never this attuned to another's touch.

"I want you," he breathed against her neck as he broke the kiss. "All of you." He licked her collarbone, then slipped lower. "You taste so sweet. Just like I imagined."

He moved closer and closer to her breasts. She found herself holding her breath in anticipation. Would she die from the pleasure? she wondered, already feeling herself tensing and shaking at the same time.

He kept his hand on her left breast, while bringing his mouth to her right. Once there, he paused until she was forced to open her eyes and look at him. With his gaze locked with hers, he touched the tip of his tongue to the sensitive tip of her nipple. To see *and* feel such exquisite sensation was more than she could stand. Without warning, her body convulsed into a wave of trembling. Deep inside her, muscles contracted. It was a release, yet not complete, for when she was still once again, she was more swollen, more damp, more ready than she'd been before.

"Shane," she breathed. "I don't know what you're doing to me."

"Loving you."

"Yes. In the best way possible. But it's so incredibly good."

That made him smile. "Isn't it supposed to be?"

"I never knew it could be like this." She had a bad feeling that she looked as shocked as she felt. "I want..."

"What?" he asked.

"Everything."

He released her long enough to peel off her panties. Perhaps his gaze lingered on the proof of her pregnancy, but she could no longer care. It was enough that his mouth returned to her breast and when he pulled her inside and suckled her, she felt the beginning of the rippling again. This time, though, he was prepared. As the first shudders crashed through her, he slid a finger into her waiting dampness. Instantly she clamped around him. He withdrew and thrust in two fingers, moving them in and out in rhythm with her contractions.

This couldn't be happening, she thought through the sensual fog in her brain. She'd never in her life climaxed more than once. But tonight, she felt as if she could do this forever. As if her body had been specifically designed to be pleasured by this man.

He released her breast and returned to kiss her mouth. She welcomed him, inviting him in, wrapping her arms around him and pulling him close. His hand moved up, his fingers searching for, then finding, the tiny knot buried under the protective fold of damp skin. He stroked it lightly, circling around before brushing over the top.

She began to shake uncontrollably. Her legs fell open and she pulled her knees up, exposing herself to him. He moved lighter, yet faster and her body collected itself for another release.

It washed over her, leaving her weak and gasping, yet still hungry with need. "Please be inside of me," she told him urgently. "Please."

"You don't have to ask me twice."

He sat up and quickly unfastened his shirt. When she put her hand on his bare chest, he cursed softly and tore the last three buttons free. In a matter of seconds he'd removed all his clothing and stood naked in front of her.

A light dusting of hair scattered across his chest. It narrowed down to his waist, then widened again just above his groin. His thighs were lean and powerful, and the essence of his maleness jutted toward her in hard readiness. She reached toward him and stroked him once. His hiss of breath told her he was as ready as she was. She opened her arms in silent invitation.

Shane knelt between her thighs. She pulled back

her knees and tried to prepare herself for the impact of his entry. Then he was pressing himself home.

Slowly, so very slowly, he slid into her. Longer and wider than she'd thought, filling her so completely that she felt the true connection of oneness. He braced his weight on his hands and stared down at her. Their eyes locked.

Then he began to move.

It was all she could do not to scream. Nothing in her previous experiences had prepared her for the pleasure of having Shane inside her. With each stroke, her body contracted and quivered around him, sending her into a spasm of perfect release. Over and over she found herself shuddering and fighting the urge to scream.

He swore. "I can see what's happening," he said. "It's in your eyes. Can I go faster?"

She didn't even realize she hadn't closed her eyes or turned away. Instead she'd left herself exposed to his gaze. But it felt right to have him know how he pleased her.

"Go faster if you'd like," she gasped. "I promise I'll be fine."

So he slipped in more quickly, thrusting and pulling back, again and again until her releases blended into one long, continuous existence. Until he slowed and stiffened and she felt himself empty inside of her. Until her body was finally calm, caught up in perfect pleasure and exhaustion. Until he shifted and held her close, his hoarse voice murmuring how very wonderful it had been. Until her heart filled with a certainty that warned her she'd gone and fallen in love with a cautious man searching for a sure thing.

When nothing in life was ever certain.

Chapter Eight

Shane couldn't remember a time when he'd felt so connected with another person. Even though his body had stopped shuddering, the remnants of pleasure still flowed through him. He could feel answering tremors in Angela as he held her close. It was as if they really had become one person for that brief period of time.

He rolled onto his side and pulled her with him so they faced each other. Patches of color stained her chest and her cheeks, and she was still breathing heavily. She opened her eyes and stared at him.

"Wow."

He grinned. "Yeah, for me, too. I didn't know making love could be like that."

She sighed. "I didn't know I was capable of reacting like that. I don't know if it was what we were doing together, or chemistry, or what, but it was as if my body had moved to another physical plane or something.''

While his ego was thrilled that he'd pleased her more than she'd ever experienced before, he was also concerned. ''Are you feeling all right? The baby—''

She cut him off with a quick shake of her head. ''The baby is fine. Despite old myths, she can't see what's happening and she's completely protected and sealed off from the outside world. I'm incredibly healthy, with no history of medical problems.'' She smiled. ''We probably rocked her to sleep.''

He shifted his hand until he could press it against the gentle rounding of her belly. ''Can you feel her yet?''

''I'm not sure. There have a been a couple of fluttery movements, but I can't help thinking I'm imagining them. I should feel something in the next couple of weeks. I've heard that it's easier to feel the baby during a second or third pregnancy, rather than a first.''

She placed her hand over his and laced their fingers together. ''I'm one of the lucky ones. I haven't been sick even a day. The only reason I thought to take a pregnancy test is that my periods have always been completely regular and I was two days late.''

''So you don't have any cravings for pickles and chocolate chip ice cream?''

''Not yet. I'll let you know if that happens.''

He stared at her, at the big, green eyes and the fading bruises on her face. As much as he tried to hold back emotion, Angela was getting to him. Yet a month ago he hadn't known she existed. "What if someone else had been assigned to you?" he asked. "What if we hadn't met?"

"Whitehorn is a small town," she said. "We would have run into each other eventually."

He supposed she was right.

"If I hadn't been a bruised amnesiac, would you still have found me attractive?" she asked, her voice teasing.

He kissed her nose. "Yes. If I'd seen you at a store or in a restaurant, I would have walked over and asked you out immediately."

"What if I'd been speeding?"

"I would have given you a ticket, then I would have asked you out."

"I couldn't bribe you with a kiss?"

She demonstrated what she would have done. Her mouth moved across his slowly, as her tongue traced the shape of his lips. Despite the fact that they'd just made love, he could feel himself wanting her again. Blood heated and headed south, filling him until he wanted to bury himself inside her.

"Would you still have given me the ticket if I'd kissed you like that?" she asked softly.

"Yeah, but I would have spent the rest of the day pretty uncomfortable."

She glanced down and saw what he was talking about, then raised her eyebrows. "Already?"

"Actually, I think we should wait for a little bit."

"All right, but I don't want to wait for long."

He rolled onto his back. She snuggled next to him and rested her head on his shoulder. After pulling the covers over both of them, he wrapped his arms around her.

It was dark outside. Lamplight spilled over most of the bed, illuminating her perfect features. He wondered what her daughter would look like and found himself hoping she was as pretty as her mother.

"Do you think about having more children?" he asked.

"Eventually. I've always wanted two or three." She pressed a kiss to his jaw. "This is probably going to sound funny and I mean it in a really good way, but I'm glad Tom's child is a girl. I think that will make it easier while I'm a single parent. Besides, even though it's not the politically correct thing to say, I'm sure if I were to marry again, my new husband would want a son of his own."

Shane frowned. He didn't like hearing about Angela marrying again. Of course it would happen. He could think of four or five guys who would snap her up in a hot minute. Not him. Never him. He wasn't in the market for permanent.

"What about you?" she asked. "Do you want enough kids for a basketball team or is baseball more your style?"

"Neither."

"You make me crazy with all your concerns

about being a good father. All the time I was with Tom, he made me dozens of promises and hardly any came true. Eventually I had to stop trusting him. But I know you're dependable. You're the kind of man who really believes his word is his bond. I know you'll never let a woman down, and certainly not a child.''

While he liked hearing the words, he didn't want her thinking he was perfect. ''I make mistakes,'' he said. ''I'll always want to do the right thing, but I might fall short.''

She grinned. ''Oh, honey, you're a guy. You're going to mess up. It comes with the territory.''

''What does that mean?''

''Just what I said.'' She settled her head on his shoulder again. ''But I'm not talking about taking out the trash or leaving socks on the floor. I'm talking about character. You won't promise that in the next town you'll stay long enough to rent a house and then say the family has to leave two weeks later. You won't take all the money in savings and buy into some company that goes out of business in less than a month or was a fake to begin with. You'll make sure that your children's future is secure.''

He didn't know how to answer that. In a couple of sentences she'd painted a picture of her life with Tom, making all she'd endured painfully clear. He wanted to go back and fix her past, even though there was no way for that to happen. He wanted to make it right when all he could do was listen and swear she would never have to worry about any of those things with him.

"What do you want to do with your life?" she asked. "To keep working for the sheriff's department?"

"I'd like to make sheriff," he said. "I like the town and the people here. We're still small enough that good law enforcement can make a difference in people's lives."

She rubbed her hand over his chest. "I think that's a great idea, but I have to admit, I can't help seeing you going into local politics."

Shane stared at her. "The city council?"

"Maybe. For a start." Her expression was impish.

He couldn't believe she'd said that. Years before, back when he and Mary had first been dating, he'd admitted that he'd sometimes dreamed about getting involved politically in Whitehorn and maybe in the state. He'd told her that he'd thought about running for public office. Mary had dismissed the idea as too impractical. He didn't have the money or the family connections. It would all be a waste of time.

"You really think I could?" he asked.

"Sure. The danger is all the single women in town will realize what a catch you are and start to try to land you." She nuzzled his neck. "But other than that, I think it would make you happy and that's what matters most."

"I don't like the idea of screaming women."

She chuckled. "I know. It's part of your charm."

"What do you want for yourself?" he asked, trying to ignore the hot dampness of her tongue against his skin. He was still aroused and very eager to take her again, but he wanted to let her rest for a while first.

"I want to teach for as long as I can, although if I really do end up with a bunch of kids, that might be a little difficult. I want to settle down and have roots. I want to belong to the community and have my kids grow up in place where they know everyone and the neighbors watch out for each other." She sighed. "On a completely different topic, describe your perfect vacation." she said. "Make that a family vacation not a romantic one."

He thought for a second. "A family, huh? Okay everyone piles into the minivan and we head off camping. The only rule is Mom doesn't do any cooking or cleaning. Instead she can spend her free time reading."

"Sounds lovely." She rubbed her hand across his chest, then started moving lower. He swallowed and tried not to notice, even though parts of him were *very* aware of her questing fingers.

"I just have one suggestion for the camping trip," she said as she trailed her fingers across his thighs, moving close to but not yet touching his arousal.

"What's that?" he asked, his voice low and strangled.

"Fishing. There should be plenty of that."

"Not a problem." Right now he was willing to promise anything, if only she would—

Then she did. She touched him, taking him in her hand and slowly moving back and forth. He surged against the gentle friction, groaning low in his throat.

"What about a romantic vacation?" Angela asked, her voice soft.

He found it difficult to concentrate on anything but her actions. Still he forced his mind to form a picture of an oceanfront getaway. Somewhere warm and private and...

"I want to go away with my husband on a regular basis," Angela said, breaking into his musings. "I think it's important to make marriage a priority. I know the children have to come first a lot of times, but without nurturing, even the best marriage can whither. I hope my husband feels the same way."

Husband. Angela would marry again. He pushed her hand away and sat up in bed.

"Shane? What's wrong?"

"Nothing."

Nothing *was* wrong, yet nothing felt right, either. Of course Angela would marry. She was that kind of woman. She was going to have a baby and any guy worth spit would love the child as much as he loved the mother. He, Shane, was going to walk away and let her get on with her life.

It made sense. What did he really know about her? They were barely more than...lovers, he thought. They were lovers and despite their relatively short acquaintance, he knew her better than he'd ever known Mary. He knew how she'd stuck by a man for longer than she should have because she'd given her word. He knew that when her life and first marriage didn't turn out the way she wanted that she gathered up the shattered bits of her dream and went to college while supporting herself. She found a new dream. He knew that even when she'd been beat up, in pain and without a scrap of memory that she'd still been thrilled to find out she was pregnant.

She was the best person he'd met. Did he really plan to let her go?

"I can't do it," he said, turning to look at her.

"What?"

"I can't let you go. I don't have a clue about being a father or a husband and I'm scared as hell that I'll screw anything up, but I can't let you run off and marry someone else."

Her green eyes brightened with something he might have dared called happiness...if he hadn't been so terrified she was going to laugh at him. But she didn't. She leaned toward him and kissed his mouth.

"I don't want to marry anyone else," she said. "Why would I? You're everything I've ever wanted."

He couldn't begin to explain how much he wanted to believe that. But it wasn't possible.

"You're wonderful," she said. "You're honorable and giving and thoughtful and very into details. Details are so important in life and in bed."

She was beautiful, he thought helplessly. He probably didn't deserve her but he wasn't sure he had a choice in the matter.

He pulled her into a sitting position. "Angela Sheppard, I love you as I've never loved anyone before. I admire your spirit and your joy. I think you're incredibly special and completely beautiful. I want to spend the rest of my life with you. Will you do me the honor of marrying me?"

Her green eyes darkened, then two tears spilled onto her cheeks. She wiped them away with the back of her hand. "Sorry," she sniffed. "I always cry when I'm happy." She flung her arms around him. "Yes, I'll marry you. I love you, too, and I want to be with you. I want to grow old with you and watch our children have children."

He couldn't believe she'd agreed. Happiness filled all of him. He pulled her close and kissed her. "Thank you. I'll love you forever. You'll never be sorry you said yes."

She kissed him. "I know."

"I'll love your daughter, as well," he promised. "As if she's my own. I know you'll want to tell her about Tom, and I think you should. But I'll be her father in every other way."

More tears rolled down her cheek. "I don't know how I got so lucky, but I'm going to hold on to you, Shane, and never let you go."

"Good."

"So when do you want to get married? Soon?"

"Sure. Tomorrow, if you'd like."

"I would like."

She stared at him. "We can't put a wedding together in a day."

"Why not? I'd like for us to get married in this

house so that we can begin making memories here. I thought maybe Nancy and Jerry would be witnesses. Unless you want something different.''

''No. That sounds perfect. I would like to marry you as soon as possible.''

He lowered his head to hers and kissed her. With her in his arms, he felt a rightness that had been missing most of his life. With Angela, he belonged.

He reached down to cup her hip. As he prepared to enter her, the phone rang.

Shane swore under his breath, then reached for the receiver. ''I'm sorry,'' he said before picking it up. ''It might be work.''

''I know,'' she said. ''It's fine.''

''McBride,'' he said into the receiver, then listened.

''Shane, I wanted to let you know that Sara Mitchell escaped from her kidnappers,'' Matt Anders, one of the deputies Shane worked with, said. ''She got away this afternoon. She seems okay, considering what she went through. Chances are those creeps are pretty steamed up about losing her and their million bucks, so the boss wanted me to tell you to make sure to not let Angela Sheppard out of your sight. He wants you two to lay low for a while. Maybe a week, until this is wrapped up.''

Shane glanced down at the lovely young woman in his arms. ''I think I can manage that,'' he said. ''We might even leave town for a few days.''

''Great idea. Just let the boss know.''

''I will. Thanks.'' He hung up the phone.

''What was that all about?'' Angela asked.

"The little girl who was kidnapped the day you were attacked managed to escape. She's fine," he added quickly when he saw the concern in her eyes. "But those men are going to be angry at having lost their chance at the ransom money. I'm under orders not to let you out of my sight for the next few days."

"Really? So that's why you mentioned leaving town."

"Exactly." He wrapped his arms around her and pressed himself against her. "I'm going to have to stay very, very close."

She gasped as he entered her. "Sort of a one-on-one kind of protection?"

"Absolutely. Only the best for the woman I love."

She started to respond, but even as her mouth formed words, he felt the pulsing of her first release. He was going to tease her about her quick response, but his own body lost itself in the pleasure of what they were doing. He couldn't think, he couldn't talk, he could only feel and be thankful that he'd been lucky enough to find her.

As weddings went, it wasn't a very big one, Angela thought as she adjusted the peach roses in her hair. There was no church, no live music, no guests except for Nancy and Jerry's two children. She wasn't even wearing a wedding gown. But Angela couldn't remember being happier or having an event in her life that felt so very right.

"You're beautiful," Nancy said, and gave Angela a hug. "And so very much in love."

"Thanks for all your help," Angela told her. "I couldn't have managed it without you."

"Hey, that's what friends are for, right? Besides, I loved the challenge of throwing a wedding together in a single day."

Nancy had indeed worked a miracle, Angela thought. When Shane had phoned her to invite her and Jerry to be their witnesses, Nancy had insisted that she help Angela make the arrangements. Fifteen minutes later she'd been at Shane's door with a notebook in one hand and a list of phone numbers in the other.

By ten they'd arranged for Angela's bouquet, flowers for the cake and a basket of rose petals for Belinda, who was going to be the flower girl. Nancy had called in a favor from a local bakery and had gotten them to agree to deliver a simple two layer wedding cake by four that afternoon. The next stop had been to take Shane's best suit to the dry cleaner's, with a promise that it would be ready by three, then they'd hit the dress shop.

There, on the sale rack, had been a pretty long-sleeved lace dress in Angela's exact size. The princess style emphasized her bust while skimming lightly over her slight tummy. Nancy had thought of disposable cameras so the event could be recorded and a romantic catered dinner for two by a local firm. Their last stop, after buying two simple gold bands, had been to Nancy's church where the secretary and part-time organist had played "The

Wedding March'' so that Nancy could record it and then play it back when Angela walked down the center of Shane's living room.

"You thought of everything," Angela said as she stared at herself in the dresser mirror. "You even did my hair."

Nancy shrugged. "I think in my last life I was a general or something. I'm great at getting it all together very quickly. Of course, the downside of that is I alphabetize my spices, which makes everyone crazy."

"I think it's charming."

Nancy smiled at her. "I hope so. I'm very glad you're marrying Shane. I know it's been quick, but something about it feels so incredibly right."

"I agree," Angela said, trying not to notice how amazing Nancy looked in a simple navy sheath dress. The woman could have made her fortune modeling.

"I told Belinda you're going to be living next to us," Nancy said, "and that you're having a little girl and she's very excited. She knows a baby will be a lot more fun than her dolls."

Angela felt tears spring to her eyes. This is what she'd always wanted—a home, friends, connections. She wanted her children to play in the neighborhood and forge relationships that would last a lifetime.

"Thank you for everything," Angela said, and hugged her.

Then Jerry knocked on the guest room door and said that it was time to get started.

Nancy went out first. Angela waited until she heard the opening of "The Wedding March" before entering the hall and heading for the living room. She'd thought she would be nervous, but she'd never been more certain in her life.

As she walked down the hall, she saw soft flickering light ahead. While she'd been dressing, Shane and Jerry had filled the living room with dozens of tiny candles. They added a soft glow to the lamplight and made Angela feel that she was in a holy place.

The minister, arranged on short notice as everything else, smiled when he caught her eye. He winked once, then nodded for her to come forward. Shane was waiting there, as well. Tall and solid, a man she knew would be at her side for the rest of their lives.

His gaze met hers. The rest of the room faded away, and in the blurriness she thought she saw images of laughing children, although there were four smiling faces in addition to hers and Shane's. She saw a big dog and several cats, heard echoes of joyous Christmas mornings to come. She saw the house—added on to and filled with a happy family. She saw her children graduate from college, then marry, except for the youngest who would always be a rebel. She saw Shane as he was now, then as he would be in his eighties, and she was at his side for the entire journey. She saw them standing together on a beach, watching the sun set, holding hands as they had every day for the past fifty years.

She came to a stop next to her husband-to-be.

When she gave Nancy her flowers, he took both her hands in his. "Are you sure?" he asked.

She looked past him to the still moving promises of what was to be. "I've never been more sure in my life," she told him. "You are where I've always wanted to be."

"You might as well kiss her now," the minister said with a grin. "I can tell that's what you're thinking of doing anyway, and if I don't let you, you'll be distracted through the entire ceremony. I like my couples paying attention."

Everyone laughed, then Shane leaned forward and touched her lips with his. The rightness of the moment grounded her. Then they turned and faced the man of God to pledge their love to each other for as long as they should live.

* * * * *

BORN IN WHITEHORN
Karen Hughes

To Leanna, Edie, Mary Anne and Lee.
For your "new" mother expertise and
your ongoing support and friendship.
Thank you.

Chapter One

"Why can't Sara talk?"

Leah Nighthawk glanced at the five-year-old seated beside her as she drove to the Hip Hop Café in Whitehorn, Montana. The sound of the girl's voice startled Leah for a moment. Jenny McCallum had been unusually quiet during the thirty-mile drive from the Laughing Horse Reservation where she'd stayed with Leah for safety's sake during the past two weeks. Anyone looking at little Jennifer would never know the child was an heiress and had almost been the victim of a recent kidnapping plot that had gone wrong.

Leah pushed her long, black hair over her shoulder as she carefully chose the right words to answer her small friend's question. "The men who took

Sara didn't hurt her, but they must have scared her before she ran away from them. Your mom and dad think she's still scared and that's why she's not talking. Maybe when she has her family and friends around her again, she'll feel safe enough to tell everyone what happened.''

Leah hoped her words had alleviated Jenny's concern. Sara Mitchell and Jenny McCallum were best friends and even looked somewhat alike with their blond hair and blue eyes. Because Sara had been wearing Jenny's coat in the schoolyard two weeks ago, the kidnappers had mistakenly taken her instead of Jenny. The McCallums had worried that the two men, who had worn ski masks during the attempt, would realize they'd kidnapped the wrong child and come after Jenny again. Leah had offered to keep the little girl with her on the reservation, knowing no one would look there, and Jenny's parents had agreed to the plan.

Leah's very round tummy brushed against the steering wheel as she turned her blue van into the parking lot of the Hip Hop Café. Snow flurries that had begun shortly after she'd left her small house on the ''res'' danced across the windshield. A welcome-home celebration for Sara had been hastily planned by the McCallums. Leah knew she was tempting fate by bringing Jenny to the party. Dr. Jeremy Winters could very well stop in. Last night he was the one who'd found Sara wandering along the road after she'd escaped from her kidnappers.

Just thinking about Jeremy made Leah's heart ache. Unbidden, memories of their night together filled her mind with vivid images, and her eyes pricked with tears. When she'd awakened in his arms almost nine months ago, she'd told him she couldn't see him again...that she was leaving Montana. But when she'd discovered she was pregnant, she'd postponed leaving and had stayed secluded on the res, working at the trading post, saving money so that when the babies were born she could leave Montana as her mother had always wanted her to do. Over and over again she'd had to remind herself that Jeremy was essentially a stranger, that she refused to be a burden to him, that one night of passion wasn't enough for her to ungratefully turn her back on the dreams her mother had nurtured for her all her life.

Jeremy was most likely making rounds at Whitehorn Memorial Hospital right now. She could slip into the Hip Hop, deliver Jenny to her parents, make sure Sara truly was unharmed, then leave before he arrived. As Leah pulled into a parking place, she anxiously checked the cars already parked there. Thankfully she didn't see Jeremy's forest-green Jeep.

Taking a deep breath, she switched off the ignition.

After she unfastened her seat belt, she protectively laid her hand on her belly and turned toward Jenny. "Before we go inside, I just want to tell you how much I enjoyed having you with me."

Jenny smiled and unbuckled her seat belt. "It was fun staying with you. I like the trading post, and practicing my Christmas pageant song with you, and you telling me stories, and…" Leaning closer, she laid her hand beside Leah's as she had quite a few times over the past two weeks. "And I like feeling the babies."

"They've been quiet today," Leah said, her overwhelmingly tender feelings toward her unborn children growing stronger by the minute. When she'd found out she was having twins, she'd been scared but also overjoyed. She'd have two babies to love.

She just wished her mother was here…she just wished…

Blinking quick tears away, she motioned outside the window. "Be careful when you get out of the van. The blacktop might be slippery." A fine layer of snow already coated the parking lot, and Leah knew Jenny's enthusiasm to get inside could make her feet slip right out from under her.

Leah opened her door and stepped onto the ground. Her hand automatically went to her back, which had been bothering her all day. She'd been feeling particularly tired, too, and just blamed it on standing on her feet at the trading post.

After her mother had been diagnosed with cancer twenty months ago, Leah had returned to the reservation from Chicago to be with her and to take care of her. She'd been fortunate to find a job as an assistant to the curator of the Native American Museum in Whitehorn. But as her mother had required more care, Leah had scaled back to part-time and finally quit during the last month of her mother's life. If Jeremy hadn't stopped in that one

evening after her mother died... If she hadn't let
him comfort her... If she hadn't foolishly made
love with him...

In spite of Leah's warning to be careful, Jenny
ran to the back door of the café, unmindful of the
snow. Leah took more care, keeping her ears alert
for the sound of any cars arriving. Once inside, she
looked around the 1950's-style diner with its
chrome and vinyl. It was decorated for Christmas,
which was less than a week away, with pinecone
wreaths, gold tinsel garlands, and mistletoe hanging
from the ceiling. Two attractive women were talking while they arranged cookies on a platter. They
both looked up when Jenny and Leah entered. Jessica McCallum, Jenny's adoptive mother, beamed
a smile at the sight of her daughter. Tall, slender
and very pretty, with sable-brown hair she wore
pulled back in a bun, Jessica was the head of the
social welfare department in Whitehorn. Danielle
Mitchell, Sara's mother, paused in her work to
watch as mother and daughter reunited once more.
Danielle, an attractive woman with auburn hair that
fell to her shoulders, had been raising Sara on her
own for the past two years since her husband had
disappeared. Leah had become friends with both
women when she'd worked at the museum where
they volunteered their time on weekends.

Jenny spotted her mother and took off at a run
across the tile floor, past the jukebox that usually
blared country-western music. Jessica opened her
arms to Jenny, enveloping her in a huge hug. Both
Jessica and her husband Sterling had visited Jenny

on the reservation and kept in constant phone contact, but it was obvious how glad mother and daughter were to be together again.

Finally Jessica straightened and came over to Leah. "I don't know how to thank you for keeping her safe."

"No thanks are necessary," Leah said. "We had fun." As she watched Jenny eat a cookie from the tray and talk with Sara's mother, Leah lowered her voice. "Is it really safe for Jenny to go home since the men haven't been caught?"

"We're putting extra security on at the ranch, and we won't let Jenny out of our sight," Jessica assured her. "We don't think they know yet they kidnapped the wrong girl. If they make a move, Sterling will be ready for them."

Sterling McCallum, Jessica's husband, was a special investigator for the sheriff's office. Leah had no doubt that he'd see that his daughter remained safe.

"I'm more concerned about Sara," Jessica said in a low voice. "I think those men said something to frighten her, and that's why she won't talk. If we can make her feel safe again and she can tell us something to help identify them—"

Jessica stopped abruptly as Danielle and Jenny joined them.

"Hi, Leah. Why don't you take off your coat," Danielle suggested. "I'm sure we can find a comfortable chair for you."

Knowing she had to avoid Jeremy, Leah said, "I

can't stay. I want to get back to the res before the storm really breaks.''

''At least have a cup of tea,'' Jessica insisted.

Before Leah could refuse, she spotted little Sara coming around the counter from the kitchen. Her long blond hair was tied in pigtails and her pretty purple sweatshirt and slacks matched. When the five-year-old saw Jenny and Leah, she broke into a huge smile. Sara didn't look any different than she had a few weeks ago. But when her gaze found Leah's, Leah saw an element of fear there that had never been in her eyes before.

Going over to Sara, Leah stooped and gave her a hug, holding on to her for a moment. ''I'm so glad you're back home again. I can't stay right now, but I'll see you again soon. Okay?'' She leaned back, and Sara just nodded.

When Leah straightened, Danielle put her arm around her shoulders. ''I swear you haven't gained any weight except for the babies.''

Leah laughed and patted her belly. ''Yes, it's all right here.''

''You be careful driving home,'' Danielle warned.

''I'll be very careful,'' Leah responded. Then, after a cautious glance around the room, she said, ''Please don't tell anyone I was here. Okay?''

Danielle and Jessica exchanged glances.

Danielle asked, ''Does this have something to do with the father of the twins?''

Leah hesitated. She hadn't told anyone who the father was. She'd decided that was best.

After an awkward pause, Jessica patted Leah's arm. "You don't have to tell us anything."

"Thank you," Leah said gratefully.

After a round of goodbyes, and a wave to Jenny's dad who was coming out of the kitchen with a tray of sandwiches, Leah headed for the door, eager to be on her way before she ran into Jeremy. Unlike most doctors who chose to make rounds in the early morning on Saturdays, Jeremy usually made his rounds in the afternoon, spending more time with his patients, listening and talking to them. He was a good doctor and had shown her mother great kindness.

And not only a good doctor, a little voice whispered in Leah's head. In her mind's eye she could picture Jeremy's wavy brown hair, his ruggedly handsome face and his green, green eyes. Their night together had been unforgettable.

But Leah didn't want to trap Jeremy Winters. She didn't want to be anyone's responsibility but her own.

As she left the Hip Hop Café, she placed one boot carefully in front of the other, walking toward her van. The weatherman was calling for at least six inches of snow by morning, maybe more. Although it meant inconvenience more often than not, Leah still loved to see the world covered in white. She was thinking about her years in Chicago, the wind and the snow, when a sharp pain stabbed her back. It was strong enough to make her grab for the door handle on her van and hold tight. Taking a slow, deep breath, she looked up at the gray sky.

This couldn't be labor. Not yet. Could it?

Her obstetrician had told her twins could be early...

Fear washed over her. She had to get back to the res, to Bessie, her mother's best friend and neighbor who had been so supportive throughout Leah's pregnancy. Bessie would know what the pain meant. After all, this could be false labor. It could be a cramp.

When the pain subsided, Leah felt relieved and climbed into the van. She switched on her headlights and drove out of the parking lot in the swirling snow. The wind had picked up and blew forcefully against the vehicle as she made her way slowly back to the res. Turning on the radio to a local station, Leah became anxious about the low visibility and turned her windshield wipers to a higher speed. But the wipers didn't seem to help as she peered through the iced glass at the mounting snow, and listened as the newscaster spoke of an accident on the other side of Whitehorn on Route 191. It was a serious one from the sound of it.

The heater struggled to keep up with dispelling the cold. Leah was reaching forward to turn the fan up a notch when a tearing contraction ripped through her and she gasped, almost losing control of the van. Somehow she managed to turn the wheel and pull off crookedly onto the shoulder of the road.

Jeremy Winters's heart had thudded crazily as his windshield wipers pushed the snow aside and he watched the woman get into the familiar blue van. She had long, silky black hair. She was also very pregnant!

When he'd first turned into the back entrance of the parking lot of the Hip Hop Café, he'd thought he recognized the older blue van.

And he had. It was Leah's. A *pregnant* Leah's.

But Leah had left the Whitehorn area! Hadn't she?

Stunned, he followed her onto the main road.

The night they'd spent together filled his mind until he had to block it out to think.

He'd never doubted that Leah would leave Laughing Horse to pursue the dream her mother had fostered. During the month he'd taken care of Leah's mother, Teresa Nighthawk had proudly told him more than once that some day Leah would be working as a curator in a museum in New York City or Washington, D.C. He knew Teresa had taken her daughter away from the reservation when Leah was small, to give her a better life, and had only returned to Laughing Horse when her own mother had suffered a heart attack. After Leah's grandmother died, Teresa had stayed in the house where she'd grown up while Leah finished college and found a job in Chicago. When Teresa learned she had cancer, she hadn't wanted Leah to come back to the res, but Leah had insisted.

At the time, Jeremy had been filling in for Kane Hunter at the Laughing Horse clinic for a month while Kane was away. Toward the end of that month, Teresa Nighthawk had died. Jeremy had returned to the res one night to check on Leah… And comfort had turned to desire. Afterward, when Leah had told him she was leaving Montana, he'd believed her. And with Kane's return to the clinic, Jeremy had had no reason to drive out to Laughing Horse again and learn differently.

Now that he thought about it, Leah's decision to leave had given him an out from pursuing his attraction to her. When he'd lost his wife and unborn child five years ago, he'd thought he'd never recover and he'd resisted relationships. The night with Leah had been an exception. He'd let down his guard with her and that was something he'd learned not to do. After all, he never again wanted to feel the pain and anguish of losing someone he cared for deeply. Instead, he'd thrown himself into his work and now his practice was his life.

Yet, he had to know if the child Leah was carrying was his. If it was, why hadn't she told him?

His thoughts and emotions whirled chaotically as he followed her onto the road to the reservation so he could confront her in private, out of the elements.

Once again memories of their night together flooded back, and he became aroused…then swore. But no sooner had the words left his mouth than Leah's van swerved erratically to the side of the road, bumping onto the shoulder. Had a tire blown? Had she skidded on the slushy road? Pulling up behind her, he switched on his flashers, got out and slammed the door.

Leah's magnificent hair hid her face as Jeremy

flung open her van door to find her doubled over behind the steering wheel.

"Leah!"

Taking short, shallow breaths, she looked up at him, her eyes filled with fear. "The babies…" Her voice caught.

"Babies?" he asked, catching the plural right away.

She nodded. "Twins. I had a sonogram and—" A moan escaped her lips as another contraction hit.

Jeremy didn't feel like a doctor now. He felt like a lover who'd been turned out into the cold, a soon-to-be-father— He cut off the thought. He didn't know that for sure.

Years of training took over as his fingers went to the pulse on Leah's wrist. Strong but fast. "How many weeks?" he asked tersely.

"Thirty-four."

Relief swept through him. Though his specialty was internal medicine, he'd treated pregnant women before sending them to obstetricians. Leah's labor was early, but not too early to put either her or the babies in danger.

"Take some deep breaths while you can," he suggested. "I'm going to call an ambulance." Pulling out his cell phone, he dialled 9-1-1, gave his location and explained the situation. To his dismay, the dispatcher told him the ambulance would be delayed. There had been an accident and it was on another call. Jeremy ordered, "Just get it here as soon as you can," then switched off the phone.

With Leah he kept his voice calm, though he was

feeling anything *but* calm. "Let's get you into the back of the van before another contraction begins." Without giving her a chance to respond, he slid open the back door then scooped her into his arms and carried her to the bench seat. Beside her in the confining quarters, he was aware of everything about her, how little her pregnancy had changed her. Her eyes were still the deepest brown velvet; her ebony hair was thick and straight and soft. She always smelled like orange blossoms and he could smell that scent now as he shrugged out of his down coat, bundled it and slipped it behind her back as a pillow.

She still looked frightened, and he tried to reassure her. "You'll be okay, Leah. Your babies will be okay. Trust me."

"I'll try," she murmured, then tensed as another contraction started.

Even without timing the contractions, Jeremy knew they were coming fast and hard, and the ambulance might not get here in time. After the contraction passed, there was moisture on Leah's brow and Jeremy suspected she was trapping all the pain inside. "Let it out, Leah. You can scream if you want to. I don't care."

She caught her breath and then looked up at him with an almost-smile. "I'm not a screamer."

He knew that was true. She had a courageous, quiet way about her that he envied.

"Can you take your coat off?" he asked. "I need something to cover you and wrap around the babies when they come."

Tugging the long coat from under her, she tried to slip her arms out. He automatically helped her. His arm was practically around her shoulders and his face close to hers— The urge to kiss her was so strong, he could barely restrain it.

But she had wanted him out of her life.

He couldn't wait any longer to ask. "Are the babies mine?"

After a moment she answered softly. "Yes."

As tension gripped her body again, he slipped her coat from her and knew they couldn't discuss this now. The stakes had suddenly gotten higher, and he thanked God he *was* a doctor, though at the moment he couldn't really do much to help her. He covered her with the coat then moved to the end of the seat.

"There's a blanket in the back," she told him. "And an old sweater. Do whatever you have to for my babies."

"*Our* babies."

She kept silent.

Snow fell onto his hair as he found the blanket and sweater in the back, but he was hardly aware of it in his concern for Leah. Retrieving his medical bag from his Jeep, he brought it into the van and shut the door. Then he helped Leah slip off her boots and undergarments and pull her jumper above her belly. He felt awkward about disrobing her, as if he were invading her privacy. But they both knew he'd have to do more than that before they were through.

Jeremy was as gentle with Leah as he could be

and when it came time to push, he knelt at her feet, encouraging her. He could see the head of one of the babies, and he urged, "Push with all your might. Let's get this one out."

Leah pushed and pushed and pushed until the head and then the shoulders were in Jeremy's hands. Finally he held a brand-new baby girl, and the feelings jumbling inside him were positively overwhelming. Checking the baby to make sure she was breathing properly, he then wrapped his daughter and laid her on Leah's tummy.

When another contraction racked Leah's body, he realized the second baby was coming quickly. After a few pushes the second birth progressed as swiftly as the first. This child was a little boy. His son!

As he laid the second baby in Leah's arms, there were tears coursing down her cheeks, and he realized his own eyes were moist. They heard the sound of the siren then, and he smiled at her. "Just in time."

"Are they okay?" she asked, concerned.

"I think they're fine. We'll know more after we get you and them checked out at the hospital."

The ambulance pulled up beside the van. In a flurry of activity, paramedics transferred Leah and the babies to the ambulance, and Jeremy wanted to climb in with them. But Leah might not want him there. She apparently didn't want him in her life. Anger pushed at all the other feelings swirling inside him as erratically as the snowflakes around him.

After the ambulance had gone safely on its way, Jeremy climbed into his Jeep and shut his eyes for a moment. He was a *father*...a father of twins. It would take Leah a while to get checked in at the hospital and settled in a room. Whether she wanted him there or not, he would *be* there. He drove to the hospital as the snow continued to fall harder.

An hour later, Jeremy stopped at Leah's room. He had made arrangements for someone to drive her van back to Laughing Horse, then he'd checked patients' charts while he waited for her to get settled. Pushing open the door, he peered inside, ready to confront the situation between them. But she was dozing, and he didn't want to disturb her. Yet he couldn't help letting his gaze linger on her. Remembering.

The desire he'd felt for Leah on their first meeting had been so elemental it had overwhelmed him. She'd come into the clinic on Laughing Horse to go over her mother's case with him, to ask what they could do to make Teresa more comfortable. Jeremy had told Leah he'd stop by to check on her mother.

When he'd made the house call, he'd been amazed by Teresa's fortitude in not wanting to take stronger medication than necessary, as well as Leah's as she'd cared for her mother. His respect and admiration for both women had grown with each successive visit, and so had his attraction to Leah. Her Northern Cheyenne heritage was evident in the beautiful contours of her face and her dark brown eyes. She was small and slender and had felt so perfect in his arms.

Forcing himself to close her door again, he headed for the nursery to see his son and daughter.

Staring down at them, he was totally taken with the babies, awed by them, until he finally picked up one and then the other. They were perfect little miracles, and he was so grateful. His chest tightened. After he checked their charts, he spoke with the pediatrician on call. Both babies were perfectly healthy at five pounds each, and ready for life in the world. Finally tearing himself away from them, he went back to Leah's room and sat in the chair beside her bed, watching her.

As if she sensed his presence, she opened her eyes and turned toward him. "Thank you."

But he didn't want her thanks. "We have to name them," he said gruffly, knowing she'd been through a lot, reluctant now to have the discussion he knew they had to have.

"I'd like to name the little girl Brooke, if that's all right with you."

He thought about it for a moment. "It's fine. And our son?"

After a moment she asked, "What would your choice be?"

"Something strong." He thought for a few moments. "How about Adam?"

"Adam," she repeated. "I like it. Adam it is."

Jeremy straightened in his chair, determined to find out why she'd kept her pregnancy from him. But before he could bring it up, a nurse wheeled in the babies. "It's time to discuss breast-feeding," she cheerfully informed the new mother.

Leah's cheeks flushed, and as much as Jeremy wanted to stay, he knew she'd be more comfortable if he left. Standing, he looked down at her. "We have a lot to talk about, but it can wait until tomorrow."

"I told the doctor I want to go home tomorrow."

"That shouldn't be a problem. The pediatrician will probably take another look at the babies in the morning. But I don't see why they can't go home with you. I'll stop for you after morning rounds."

"You don't have to. I can call Bessie." Her voice was soft but sure.

Bessie Whitecloud was Leah's next-door neighbor and had been her mother's best friend. But he wasn't going to leave this responsibility to someone else. "I'm taking you and the babies home tomorrow, Leah." Before she had a chance to argue with him, he went to the door, took one last look at Brooke and Adam and then headed down the hall.

Snow was still falling when Leah looked out her hospital window at the cottonwoods heavy with white the next morning. Jeremy was going to take her home. So many conflicting emotions washed over her from the events of the past night. She was amazed that Jeremy had found her and relieved he'd been there to deliver the babies. She remembered how he'd towered over her so strong and determined.

That's exactly why she hadn't told him about her

pregnancy. Because he was so strong and determined, she was afraid he wouldn't let her do what she needed to do. Decisions she would make about her future had to do with leaving her past behind and reaching for the kind of life her mother had envisioned for her. There were precious ties to her mother in the house on Laughing Horse, but Teresa Nighthawk had struggled valiantly for years to free her from any ties to the reservation. When Leah thought about feeding Brooke and Adam for the first time, how she'd experienced great surges of love and protectiveness as they'd suckled at her breasts, she appreciated even more all the sacrifices her mother had made for her.

There was a quick rap on her door and Jeremy stepped inside, all six-feet-two-inches of him. He was lean, his shoulders broad, his muscles honed, and she didn't even know from what. They'd had many conversations during the month he'd cared for her mother, but they'd mostly concerned his work, her life on the reservation, the history of the Northern Cheyenne. He'd been curious and interested, and whenever Teresa Nighthawk had told him stories, Leah had learned more herself.

Jeremy was wearing jeans and high shoe boots this morning, and Leah could see a flannel shirt underneath his blue down jacket. She felt drawn to him in a man-woman way that definitely shouldn't be on her mind this morning.

But as his gaze passed over her corduroy jumper that now hung loosely, she wished his mere presence didn't make her breath catch. Instead, she concentrated on his words as he said, ''I managed to get hold of the owner of the Children's Corner this morning, so I have car seats, something she called buntings, and diapers, in case you weren't stocked up yet.''

Already he was taking responsibility for her. ''Thank you,'' she murmured. ''I spoke with the nurses about wrapping the babies in blankets, but buntings will be much better. I'll reimburse you for everything when we get home.''

His voice was deep and gruff. ''You'll do no such thing. Brooke and Adam are my responsibility as much as yours.''

She knew Jeremy was the type of man who fulfilled his obligations. There would be no argument with him about this. Yet she wanted to make something very clear. ''I don't expect you to care for the babies. I don't expect anything from you.''

He raked his hand through his hair. ''Obviously, or you would have told me I was about to become a father.'' There was an edge to his voice, an undertone of anger, but before Leah could address it, the nurse wheeled the babies in and it was time to get ready to go.

At least eight inches of snow had fallen, covering Whitehorn and the surrounding area, but the main road had been plowed. Leah knew Jeremy hadn't said everything he needed to say, and the tension was high between them as he maneuvered through the still-falling snow, concentrating on his driving. They could get an additional six inches if this kept up.

When they reached the res, none of the snow-covered dirt roads had been plowed. They almost got stuck once, but Jeremy's expertise in handling the Jeep got them going again. Still, as they reached Leah's house, they both breathed a sigh of relief. "I might never get out of here again," he muttered.

"Mack—over at the gas station—has a pickup with a plow on the front. He'll try to get the roads open as soon as he can."

Jeremy unfastened his seat belt. "Give me your key. I'll take the twins inside and then come back and get you."

"I'll be fine," she murmured.

His impatience with her answer showed as his brows drew together and his jaw set. "Listen, Leah. You had twins less than twenty-four hours ago. You might think you're a superwoman, but when Adam and Brooke are crying at the same time and you don't know whether to feed or diaper first, you'll know you're not. Stay put until I come and get you."

This was a side of Jeremy she had never seen and didn't know if she liked. "No one's ever given me orders like a dictator, Jeremy. Don't think *you* can start now." Her quiet but firm tone told him she wouldn't be bossed or bullied.

"Fine, have it your own way," he said as he opened his door and stepped outside.

First Jeremy broke a path to the front door, so walking it with the twins would be easier. Then he carried Brooke inside, coming back a few moments later for Adam. In the meantime, Leah climbed out, but the large steps she had to take were hard for her. Jeremy came down the porch steps and met her a few feet from the Jeep. "You want to do this the hard way or the easy way?"

"The easy way," she said, looking up at him apologetically.

Sweeping her into his arms, he carried her to the porch. His chest was hard against her. His cologne was a musky pine. His lips were sensual and...

He set her down.

When she crossed the threshold into the house, she let its familiar ambience distract her from her awareness of Jeremy. The blue-and-tan tweed sofa with removable pillows at its back was old now, but still comfortable. She'd slept there when she and her mother had returned to the res to visit her grandmother. Above it hung a shield of rawhide, decorated with feathers and trade beads. The pine coffee table and end tables had been crafted by Bessie's husband, Joe, as had the two cradles sitting side by side beside a set of bookcases topped by a snapping turtle shell. On the wall above those hung a circle of life mounted on a prayer wheel. A worn armchair was angled beside the black woodstove in the corner. To Leah's surprise, the living room felt cooler than usual. Suspecting the problem, she went to the lamp by the sofa and turned it on, but no light shone. She guessed the electricity hadn't been off long, otherwise it would be a lot colder in the house.

"The electricity's out," she said. "I'll have to get the woodstove fired up." Going over to her children, she looked down at them tenderly. She'd fed them before they'd left the hospital and for the moment they seemed to be content. Fortunately she had been getting ready for them for the past few months and had almost everything she needed from an infant tub to diapers.

"I'll get the stove going," Jeremy decided. "Is the wood out back?"

She nodded. By the time she'd taken off her coat and unzipped Brooke's bunting, there was a rap on the door. "Come in," she called.

"I was so worried about you. The van came back and you didn't. What—"

Bessie Whitecloud stopped short as she stepped inside. Leah's surrogate mother was plump, wore her gray-streaked black hair short around her face, and always had a mischievous twinkle in her eye. Her gaze now, however, was filled with concern.

Picking up her daughter, Leah carried her over to Bessie. "This is Brooke." Motioning to the other cradle, she said, "And that's Adam."

"Oh, my goodness!" Bessie exclaimed. "You had the babies." Taking Brooke from Leah, she cuddled her close and softly crooned to the little girl.

Just then the back door opened and Jeremy, carrying an armful of wood, came in from the kitchen.

"Well," Bessie said, looking expectantly at Leah. "Hello, Dr. Winters."

"Hi, Bessie." He smiled at her. "What do you think of my daughter?"

"She's absolutely beautiful." Walking over to

the other cradle, she peered down at Adam. "And he's going to be as handsome as his dad." With a self-satisfied smile, Bessie admitted, "I thought you might be the father."

Leah was totally astonished.

Bessie went on. "Leah wouldn't say, but I didn't know who else it could be. Do you two want me to keep this hushed up?"

Jeremy dumped the wood by the stove. "Absolutely not. I'm proud to claim my children." Opening the stove, he arranged some logs inside.

Ashamed and embarrassed, Leah felt guilty for having gotten herself into this predicament. Jeremy blatantly proclaiming his fatherhood didn't help. When she'd discovered she was pregnant, she'd gone to Bessie, not knowing who else to confide in, worried about how others in their small community would see her. But Bessie had declared that Leah had gained everyone's respect by the tender care she had taken of her mother and if she stayed at Laughing Horse, she might see a few frowns of disapproval at her pregnancy, but anyone who knew her would support her. Still, Leah had felt awkward, and did now, too.

Scooping up Adam, Leah held the baby in her arms, then leaned down and placed a tender kiss on his forehead. "I'm going to take Adam with me to nurse. Will you stay for a few minutes?" she asked the older woman.

"I'll look in on you before I leave," Bessie assured her.

Unnerved by Jeremy's presence in her house and

his proprietary attitude toward the twins, Leah took Adam into the bedroom, knowing as soon as Bessie left, she and Jeremy were going to have to face the subject of his fatherhood and what they were going to do about it.

Chapter Two

As soon as Leah took Adam into her bedroom and closed the door, Jeremy turned to find Bessie watching him. "What is it, Bessie?"

"I'm not sure how to say this, Dr. Winters—"

"Jeremy," he corrected her.

"All right. Jeremy. When Leah came back to Laughing Horse, she wasn't accepted here simply because she was born here. She was accepted because she earned that acceptance by her attitude toward everyone, her kindness, her sacrifice in taking care of her mother."

"What are you trying to tell me?"

"I understand that you're proud to be a father, but if you announce it publicly, without a promise of marriage, you're going to make Leah very uncomfortable. The old ways are still very evident here.''

Jeremy knew that was true. When he'd first taken over Kane's duties at the clinic, he'd been met by suspicion. Until he'd proven he was a good doctor. Until he'd proven he *wanted* to be caring for the Northern Cheyenne on the reservation.

"Since I didn't know Leah was pregnant, all of this has been a shock. Suddenly I'm the father of twins. We haven't made any decisions yet, but I'll keep in mind what you said.''

Bessie studied him pensively, then after stopping in Leah's room to tell her to call if she needed her, she left.

Jeremy carefully picked Brooke up from the cradle, looking down at the little girl in awe of what he and Leah had created. Her hair was the darkest brown rather than black like her brother's. Her eyes were dark, her complexion lighter than Adam's. He marveled at her perfect little hands and rubbed his index finger gently against her knuckles. Then he peeked into the bedroom.

The house was small, consisting of a living room, eat-in kitchen, and two bedrooms. It looked as if Leah intended to keep the babies in the bedroom with her instead of turning the spare room into a nursery. Maybe because she intended to leave soon after the twins' birth. That thought made him push the bedroom door open farther.

He found Leah in a chair by the window, breast-feeding Adam, humming softly to him. She'd changed into a long-sleeved navy dress that opened down the front, and high socks with moccasins. She had the blanket arranged in such a way that both her breast and the baby's head were hidden from his view.

"Do you mind if I come in?" he asked, determined to face the issues between them, determined to control his desire for this twenty-six-year-old beautiful woman who had tried to shut him out of her life.

She stopped humming and looked disconcerted. Then she made sure the blanket was covering her. "You can come in."

She was still modest with him even though he'd kissed her body every place imaginable. Maybe she wished that night had never happened. But it had, and now they were going to deal with it.

Holding Brooke, he sat on the bed a few feet from Leah. "Why didn't you tell me I was going to be a father?"

Lifting her gaze to his, she said, "We spent one night together, Jeremy. We're essentially strangers. I didn't want to burden you."

Though he felt anger rising inside him, he was aware of the infant in his arms and kept his tone tempered. "That's rubbish. Children are only a burden when their parents don't want them. I do want them, more than you know, and I intend to be a father, even if you move to Tombouctou. Are you going to leave?"

Leah adjusted the blanket. "I sent résumés out early in the month."

Jeremy's heart gave a lurch. "Why must you go?"

Leah turned to gaze out the window, pensively watching the falling snow. Finally turning back to him, she explained. "When my father died, my mother took me to Chicago so I could have a life away from the res—from the poverty, the unemployment, the sense of being trapped. She wanted me to be a success and reach for a dream far from here."

Leah stopped for a few moments then went on. "She sacrificed everything for me, Jeremy. She went for a year at a time without seeing her own mother, without having close friends as she did here. More than anything, I've always wanted to be a curator in a museum in New York City or Washington, D.C. I can be that. I can do that for her. I can make sure her sacrifice meant something."

"What about yourself, Leah? What about your children? What about me being a father to them? How am I going to do that if you move to New York or Washington?"

"You can see them whenever you want."

But they both knew that wasn't true—not if she moved away. The sudden silence was broken when Brooke began fussing, then out-and-out crying. Apparently she was hungry, too.

Leah lifted Adam to her shoulder to burp him, but when she did, the blanket fell and her breast lay exposed. Jeremy stared at its fullness, at the nipple that had given Adam nourishment. Feelings inside him ran riot and he realized they were deeper than sexual, deeper than anything he had ever felt.

Leah quickly covered herself and it was obvious she was a bit awkward with the whole procedure, but she was a natural mother. He could tell.

As Adam burped, she met Jeremy's gaze again, her cheeks flushed. "If you take Adam, I'll feed Brooke. He might need to be changed. I know you probably want to leave—"

Attempting to lay Brooke in her lap, he found it was difficult juggling twins, especially with his awareness of Leah's bare breast just under the blanket. And as much as he tried to prevent it, in the exchange of babies, his arm brushed her and she jerked away. Had he hurt her? Nursing mothers were often very tender at first. Or maybe she just didn't want *him* touching her.

Putting Adam to his shoulder, he said, "I'm not going anywhere, Leah. First of all, I doubt if I could get the Jeep off the res. And second, I'm not leaving you here with two newborns and no electricity. I'm going to stay and help whether you want me to or not. At least until the electricity comes back on. After I change Adam, I'll put him in his cradle while I shovel snow. It would be a good idea when you're finished with Brooke, if you put your feet up and rest, too."

The flare of spirit in Leah's eyes said she didn't like him telling her what to do. But before she could protest, he took Adam into the living room.

Leah fed Brooke, awed by the miracle of her daughter, awed by her all-consuming feeling of

love. After she'd swaddled the baby and checked
on Adam now asleep, she pushed the cradles near
the sofa where it was warmer. She was so tired and
confused by Jeremy's presence in her house. He
wanted to claim fatherhood more vigorously than
she'd ever imagined he would.

Rumors had circulated about him last March before he had taken over Kane's duties at the clinic.
She knew he was a widower, but that was about all
she knew. Had he and his wife longed to have children? Is that why he was determined to be a father
to Brooke and Adam?

After she tenderly kissed both Brooke's and
Adam's foreheads, Leah stretched out on the sofa.
She needed to get her energy back. She needed to
feel strong for whatever came next. She needed to
stop remembering Jeremy's expression as he'd
looked at her naked breast.

It seemed like only a few minutes later when she
sensed someone close and opened her eyes to see
Jeremy crouched beside her at the sofa. The top
button of his flannel shirt was open at the neck and
she could glimpse the brown, curling hair she'd run
her fingers through almost nine months ago. Vi-
sions of that night still danced in her dreams. Now
with the scent of his musky cologne mixing with
the male scent of physical labor, all of her senses
came alive.

"I'm going to walk to the convenience store and
get you some groceries. Will you be all right alone
for a little while?"

Nervous about being alone with the babies, but

determined not to depend on Jeremy, she pushed herself up against the arm of the sofa so she was sitting at eye level with him. "I'll be fine. I'll have to feed them again in about an hour if not before. That's mostly what I'll be doing for the next few weeks."

"And changing diapers," he said with a smile.

"Yes, that, too." She started to slide her legs from the sofa. "I'll get you some money—"

"No, you won't. I'll take care of it."

"Look, Jeremy..."

"Now don't get all independent on me again. I'm just going to buy you a few groceries. Is there anything specific that you want?"

She simply didn't have the strength to fight with him today, but she wouldn't let him take care of her and the babies as if she couldn't do it herself. "There's a list on the refrigerator of the foods I shouldn't have since I'm breast-feeding. Other than that, I *am* partial to strawberry ice cream."

His green eyes twinkled with amusement and he was incredibly near. The fluttering in her tummy didn't have anything to do with the babies anymore. When he leaned a little closer to her, her breath almost stopped and she thought he was going to kiss her.

Instead he murmured, "I'll buy a little bit of everything," then got to his feet and towered over her. "Do you have any flashlights or battery-powered lanterns for when it gets dark, if the electricity isn't back on?"

"I have an oil lamp in the kitchen and some candles."

"Are you warm enough?"

The woodstove had made the room cozy, but it was Jeremy's presence that made her blood run fast and brought a flush to her cheeks. "I'm fine. And don't hurry to get back. I'm old enough to take care of myself, you know."

"That's what I'm afraid of," he muttered. Then he went to the refrigerator for her list, snatched his coat from the back of the chair, pulled on his gloves, and after a last look at his twins, left the house.

Leah was dozing again when Jeremy returned and carried grocery bags to the kitchen. After she checked the babies and tenderly brushed their hair from their foreheads, she went to help Jeremy put the groceries away.

Glancing at her as she put the milk in the refrigerator, Jeremy said, "Down at the store, I heard that Mack was having trouble with his pickup. He hopes to have it fixed by tonight." With a nod to the tray of chicken he'd bought, he asked, "How about baked chicken, baked potatoes, and carrots for supper?"

It was obvious that he was determined to take care of her. At least for today, she'd let him. "That sounds wonderful. Where did you learn to cook?"

"My mother. She insists a man who can read can cook."

Leah laughed. "She sounds like a very reasonable lady. Does your father cook?"

"No. He usually eats out or shops at the deli. They're divorced. Have been since I was ten."

"I'm sorry to hear that. Do you have any brothers or sisters?"

"Nope. And although there are advantages to being an only child, I'm glad Adam and Brooke will have each other."

Leah would have probed into Jeremy's background further, but suddenly a beeping sound came from the pager on his belt. He checked it. "I have to call my service. I can put the rest of this away when I'm done."

"Jeremy, it won't hurt me to move around a little and do something."

With an arch of his brows, he took the receiver from the phone on the wall and dialed in a number. Leah couldn't help listening as she put carrots into the vegetable bin.

"She's never happy when somebody else takes over for me," obviously speaking about one of his patients. "I'll give her a call. And Elise, too." After punching in another set of numbers, Jeremy spoke to his patient for a few minutes, asking what medication she had taken today, then telling her she could increase one medication while stopping another. Afterward, he asked about her husband and talked with her for a few minutes.

Leah admired his kindness and patience and could see again why he was such a good doctor. Opening cupboards, she stored the prepared foods he'd bought. When he dialed another number, she heard him greet the woman named Elise with enthusiasm.

Maybe a little too much enthusiasm, Leah thought, then scolded herself.

But as she listened to this conversation, it was obvious Jeremy was working with the woman on a fund-raiser for the hospital and sounded as if he enjoyed it. The annoyance Leah felt made her examine her feelings, and she found herself wondering what Elise looked like. Closing the cupboard with a snap, she told herself it didn't matter and she had no right to be even a little bit jealous.

After Jeremy finished with his calls, he checked the range. "It's a good thing you have a gas oven or we'd have to have canned soup on top of the woodstove."

"I can mix up some corn bread," she said.

With a shake of his head, he came over to her. "What am I going to do with you?"

Her heart thumped harder as she looked up at him. "I'm not an invalid, Jeremy."

Reaching out, he brushed her hair behind her ear, letting his fingers glide through it as if he relished touching it. "No, you're not. But you've just gone through the most wondrous ordeal a woman can go through and you need to recover from it."

With his hand on her shoulder and his body so close to hers, she felt she needed to recover from more than the birth of her twins. She needed to recover from seeing Jeremy again, having him around, talking with him. After that night when she'd told him she didn't want to see him again, she'd denied to herself that she'd missed him. But now she couldn't. She felt the constant pull toward him. His green eyes were mesmerizing; the shadow line of his beard was beginning to show, and she wanted to touch him so badly her fingers tingled. His hands slid into her hair again, to the nape of her neck, and he held her as he bent his head. His lips on hers made her senses reel, her heart quiver, her body tremble. His tongue swept into her mouth, filling her with a longing that she'd forgotten, a longing that had begun over the course of a few hours on one dark night.

But then he retreated and stepped away. His voice was husky when he said, "Marry me, Leah."

Stunned, she backed up a few steps. "You're not serious."

"Yes, I am. I want to take care of you and the twins."

She shook her head. "I can't marry you. I won't be someone else's burden. I'm going to take care of the twins myself."

"Be reasonable."

"I *am* being reasonable. Duty isn't a good basis for marriage."

His eyes sparked with desire. "We have more."

One of the babies started crying then.

"I have to look after them," she said as an excuse to end the conversation. But as she turned, he caught her arm.

"This discussion isn't closed, Leah."

She could see the determination again in his eyes, but she knew she would never marry him for anything less than the happily-ever-after kind of love she'd always wanted and dreamed of. Maybe Jeremy didn't think the discussion was over but she knew it was, and she could be just as determined as he could.

A short while later Jeremy brought her a sandwich and a glass of milk as she sat on the sofa feeding Brooke. When Adam began fussing, Jeremy picked him up and held him on his shoulder as he walked around the room and ate a sandwich of his own.

"Do you have a pacifier?" he asked.

"On the dresser in the bedroom."

As he went to get it, Leah realized there was something about Jeremy holding the tiny baby on his strong shoulder that made her stomach somersault and a warm feeling squeeze her heart.

During the rest of the afternoon and evening, Leah tried to forget about the kiss, tried to forget the feelings it evoked, tried to forget she didn't want someone taking care of her. The babies slept through supper, and Jeremy didn't return to the subject of marriage. Rather they talked of Sara and what had happened to her and how they hoped both little girls would be safe now. Yet they knew Jenny and Sara wouldn't be truly safe until the kidnappers were caught.

After supper, Leah read a child-care book while Jeremy insisted on doing the dishes by himself. But then both babies became fussy and the two of them rocked and cajoled and paced until the infants finally settled down around midnight. The bedroom had warmed up, too, from the heat of the stove, and Jeremy carried the cradles into it. After making sure both babies were sleeping, Leah changed into her nightgown and robe, then stood in the doorway watching Jeremy page through the child-care book by the light of a battery-operated lantern he'd bought that morning.

As if sensing her there, he turned. Rising to his feet, he carried the lantern with him and stopped in front of her. "You'd better sleep while you can. I'll keep the fire going."

"I want to thank you again for what you did for me last night...for what you did today. I'm very grateful."

"I'm a doctor. I would have helped any woman in the predicament you were in last night. And today...well, I'm the twins' father. I've wanted kids for so long—" He stopped abruptly, and Leah thought she saw pain in his eyes. Deep pain.

"Anyway," he said, "I'll keep watching the stove. You keep watch over the babies and if you need me, yell." Then he tipped her chin up and put the lightest of kisses on her lips before moving away.

Leah held her fingertips to her lips for a few moments and slid into bed, thinking about Jeremy on the sofa.

Bedlam broke loose two hours later when both twins began crying. Leah didn't feel adept at feeding two babies at once, besides the fact that she wanted to give them individual attention. Already she realized that Brooke was the faster eater, so she picked her up first. When she looked up, she saw Jeremy coming into the room, the top button of his jeans unfastened, his bare chest drawing her attention as she put Brooke to her shoulder.

Assessing the situation in an instant, Jeremy picked up Adam and the pacifier. "I'll change him and walk him until you're finished with Brooke."

She was amazed at how easily Jeremy handled the twins. Was it because he was a doctor? As she heard Adam still fussing in the living room, her stomach tied up in knots. She felt helpless with both twins needing her at the same time. She'd have to get used to it, but she was incredibly grateful that Jeremy had stayed.

Leah fed and soothed while Jeremy walked and talked to the twins as if they could understand everything he was saying. Neither of the babies wanted to go back to sleep and both cried, but somehow Jeremy and Leah worked together through the dead of night, giving each other encouragement, learning together what worked and what didn't. When the twins finally fell back to sleep, it was after 4:00 a.m.

"Quick, you'd better climb into bed and get a nap before they wake up again," Jeremy teased.

She smiled, but as her gaze fell on his bare chest, she suddenly wished she could be held in his arms. Yet that wouldn't be a solution to anything. Desire couldn't be a substitute for true bonds and deep love.

Yet as Jeremy's gaze traced the vee of her pink

silky nightgown, then moved up to her lips, she realized the one night they'd shared had been more than desire-filled on her part.

The silence in the house intensified the vibrations between them as Jeremy reached for her— Then he dropped his hand. "I'll check the stove. You get some sleep."

When he would have turned away, she asked, "Have you been around babies much? You seem to know exactly what to do."

He looked down at her, and she again sensed deep pain inside of him. But then the unguarded moment was gone and he smiled wryly. "Little people aren't all that different from grown-up people. Good night, Leah."

The twins were still sleeping at daybreak when Leah heard Jeremy stirring in the living room. She noticed her alarm clock was flashing and realized the electricity must have come back on. After she donned her robe and brushed her teeth, she found Jeremy scrambling eggs in the kitchen.

"Good morning," he said.

His hair was damp and she suspected he'd gotten a shower. "You didn't have to make breakfast."

"You need your energy if you're going to handle twins by yourself today. I have to get to the hospital for morning rounds, but I can come back afterward—"

"No."

He glanced over his shoulder at her.

"I mean, I don't want to seem ungrateful, but I

have to learn to handle the twins by myself. Your being here last night was a great help, but now I have to take over."

"I see. So you want to prove to yourself that all they need is a mother?" His voice carried an impatient edge.

She couldn't tell him he was wrong. "If I leave Montana, I have to be able to cope on my own."

Her words hung between them as they quickly ate breakfast. When Jeremy would have done the dishes, she insisted that she would do them herself. He looked in on the twins before he put on his jacket, and she followed him to the door. Leah could see a single lane had been plowed up the street, but Jeremy would have to dig his car out.

"I have a snow shovel out back," she offered.

"I have one in the Jeep. It won't take me long to dig out. The snow's light."

As he looked down at her, his eyes became as deep a green as she'd ever seen them. "I know you want to stand on your own two feet, but there's a time to be proud and a time to put pride aside. You might not want to marry me, but that's not going to affect the kind of father I intend to be. Babies change quickly and grow too fast, and I'd rather not miss any of it. So whether you want my help or not, I'm going to be checking in every day to make sure you're all right and to make sure the twins have everything they need. And I want you to call me if you need me. Will you do that?"

She would do what was best for her babies and

if that meant calling Jeremy, she would. "I'll call you *if* I need you."

Taking her chin in his hand, he bent his head. His lips sealed to hers in a fiery kiss that reminded her she had needs as a woman. Abruptly ending the kiss, he broke away.

She felt dazed as she gazed into his eyes.

"I'll stop in again tonight," he said.

She just nodded.

Turning, he left her house and started for the Jeep.

Leah closed the door wondering if all women felt confused after childbirth, wondering if all women felt as if their world had been turned upside down.

Monday passed in a blur for Leah. Adam was fussy all day and hardly slept. While she fed Brooke, her son cried and she felt guilty for not being able to give him the attention he needed. When she fed him, he still fussed and cried, and she began to worry. There was no break for a nap, and it seemed as if she hadn't slept in a week. Bessie stopped in after working a shift at the trading post, but Leah didn't want to burden her with caring for babies. Still, Bessie took care of her later in her own way by sending a casserole over for Leah's supper.

Around 8:00 p.m., Jeremy called to tell her he'd planned to be there by then, but something had delayed him at the hospital. Leah assured him she had everything under control…but she didn't. She was up all night with Adam and, by Tuesday morning, she was exhausted and worried sick. When she called the pediatrician who had checked the babies before they d left the hospital, she learned he'd gone away for the Christmas vacation. Another doctor was covering his practice. But a few hours later, he hadn't returned her call and Adam was still crying.

It was around two in the afternoon when she called Jeremy, telling herself not to sound like a hysterical new mother. Trying to stay calm and composed, her voice catching only slightly, she told him she was worried about Adam and didn't know what to do.

After listening, Jeremy responded immediately. "I'll call in a favor. Hold tight. I'll get right back to you."

He was as good as his word. In five minutes her phone rang and she answered it with Adam on her shoulder. Jeremy said, "Dr. McGruder will be there in an hour. He's a gastroenterologist and good with kids. I'll be there as soon as I can."

Leah had never expected such special treatment. "I don't know how to thank you..." Her voice broke.

"You don't have to thank me. They're my babies, too," he said to her. "We'll get this worked out."

Grateful when Dr. McGruder, a balding gentleman in his late fifties, knocked on her door, she answered all of his questions about her diet, as well as questions about Adam. He was examining her son on the kitchen table when Jeremy arrived.

"Well, George, what do you think?" Jeremy asked him.

Speaking to Leah as well as Jeremy, the doctor said, "I think we should put him on a special formula. And from the looks of this young lady here, it won't hurt to have him on a bottle so someone else can feed him."

"Are you sure that's what's best?" Leah asked, hating the idea of not breast-feeding Adam.

"Adam has already benefited from your breast milk. And you can give your son just as much attention as your daughter. It will simply be different. If Adam takes to this formula, we'll know it's what he needs. Let me write it down for you."

Jeremy took the slip of paper from the doctor's hand. "I'll go into Whitehorn and get whatever you need."

Too frazzled to argue, Leah felt like having a good cry, but she wouldn't give in to the urge. She didn't want Jeremy to think she couldn't cope. Before the doctor left, she told him to bill her for the visit, but he shook his head. "Jeremy and I are friends, and we do each other favors when we need it. Don't you worry about it."

For more than an hour, Leah rocked and walked Adam until Jeremy returned with the special formula and bottles that had nipples designed for infants who were breast-fed. He'd also bought a breast pump. Somehow Brooke slept through all the commotion. After they readied a bottle, Leah sat in the rocker with Adam. It took him a while to catch on to sucking from the bottle, but soon he did. Not long after, he fell asleep in her arms.

"Using the pacifier probably helped him adapt to the bottle." Jeremy gently brushed Adam's chin with his thumb. "He's exhausted. And you are, too."

Tears began rolling down Leah's cheeks then, and she had no control over them.

Taking Adam from her, Jeremy laid him in his cradle. Then he crossed to Leah and pulled her up from the rocker. "Come here," he said gently, and folded her into his arms.

His strength seeped into her, and she held on to Jeremy as if he were a life preserver in a stormy sea. Finally she leaned away. "I don't want Adam to feel neglected."

"He won't, and if the formula works, it will be easier on both of you. I'll stay the night and feed him. You can put Brooke in bed with you and get some sleep. You need a break, Leah. I called Bessie while you were feeding Adam. She'll take care of the twins so you can get out for a while tomorrow afternoon."

"But I have to feed Brooke…"

"I promise we won't be gone long. You can feed her right before we leave. She already seems to be on a schedule. We'll be back before you have to feed her again, and I have my cell phone in case she needs you sooner. Bessie can call us, and I can have you here in fifteen minutes. Or you can express milk for a bottle."

"But, Jeremy—"

"An hour and a half...two at the most. They'll be okay without you, Leah, really they will."

Her tears had released the tension that had built up inside her from worrying about and caring for the twins. But a different kind of tension started building as Jeremy still held her in the circle of his arms. "Where are you taking me?" she asked.

He smiled. "It's a surprise. I have to go into my office tomorrow morning, but then I'll pick you up after lunch. Around one." Gazing down at her, he suggested, "Listen."

Both twins were asleep for the first time in more hours than Leah could count. She smiled at him, wondering if he was trying purposefully to make himself indispensable to her.

Because if that was his intent, he was succeeding.

Across from Jeremy in the Jeep the following afternoon, Leah sat quietly. He wondered if she was thinking about the twins or maybe about Christmas only two days away. She'd been quiet ever since he'd picked her up. But she looked rested and relaxed and that's what was important. She'd slept last night between Brooke's feedings. When he'd gotten up to feed Adam, he'd looked in on her and couldn't help standing there watching for a while. She'd been curled on her side, her long black hair splayed across the pillow, Brooke beside her. Finally the deep yearnings inside him had made him turn away and go back to the sofa.

All of his life, Jeremy had wanted a large family. He'd been loved by both his parents, but separately.

His mother had remarried and moved to England; his father lived in Oregon. He'd spent winters with his father and summers with his mother. While his parents were married, Jeremy had hated their fights. But after their divorce, he'd hated their coldness toward each other more, and he'd dreamed of a whole family with strong bonds and deep caring that were a glue that lasted a lifetime.

His wife, Gwen, had also wanted several children. She'd wanted nothing more than to stay at home and care for them. If only she'd waited for him to go shopping with her for baby furniture that day. If only...

No more if-only's. Leah and Adam and Brooke could be the family he'd always dreamed of.

After he turned off the main road, Jeremy drove up a hill and turned into the plowed long driveway. Leah was peering through the frosted window, and he tried to see his home through her eyes. The cedar-sided, multilevel house nestled between cottonwoods and pines. With snowcapped mountains rising up behind it in the distance, there was a rustic country look to the setting that always gave him a sense of peace.

Pulling up in front of the garage, he braked and switched off the ignition. When he shifted toward Leah, he said, "Welcome to my home."

"Oh, Jeremy, it's lovely. How long have you lived here?"

"Almost five years." They'd begun building it soon after Gwen had learned she was pregnant.

Before Leah unfastened her seat belt, Jeremy

climbed out and hurried around the Jeep to open
her door. She smiled up at him, and he didn't think
she'd ever looked prettier. She'd braided her hair
into one long plait down her back and tied it with
red ribbon, her bangs fluffed softly on her forehead.
She was wearing a denim skirt and red blouse with
boots today, and he couldn't believe how much he
desired her, how much he wanted to keep her in his
life.

Offering her his hand, he helped her down, then
walked with her to his front door, which was shel-
tered by a small portico. He unlocked the door and
let her precede him inside.

There was the warm glow of polished wood everywhere—from the hardwood floors to the rich-
grained wide trim bordering the doors and windows. The main floor was open space. Bookshelves
divided the living room from the dining area, and
the kitchen lay beyond. The rooms were done in
blues and greens and natural colors that blended
with the wood. Long casement windows let in
bright sunlight. To the right of the foyer, a few steps
led downstairs to a family room and upstairs to the
bedrooms.

"This is beautiful."

"Let me take your coat. I'll light a fire, then give
you a tour."

His fingers lingered on her collar and brushed her
neck. She looked over her shoulder at him, and he
could see she was as aware of him as he was of
her, especially now that they were alone and without their twins requiring attention. He would have

kissed her then, but he didn't want her to think he'd brought her here for that.

After he hung their coats in the foyer closet and set a match to kindling under the log, he motioned to the few steps leading upstairs. Berber carpet lined them and the upstairs hallway. First he showed her the two guest rooms and bath, then he guided her to the master suite.

Her eyes grew wide as she took in the four-poster, king-size bed, the double dresser and chest with hand carvings on the drawers. There was a sitting area with a love seat, oval coffee table and wing chair. Beyond that she could glimpse a large bathroom. "It has a whirlpool tub," he noted.

But Leah didn't seem interested in examining it. Instead she wandered around the room and stopped by the dresser. Then she picked up a sterling-silver picture frame. "Is this your wife?"

"Yes."

"She's very pretty. What was her name?"

"Gwen."

Still holding the picture, Leah asked, "When did you lose her?"

"Five years ago."

Gently, Leah set the frame back down. "How?"

Memories came rushing back and he suddenly felt as if he had something to protect. "It was an accident, but I don't want to talk about it, Leah. That's not why I brought you here."

Crossing the room, she stood in front of him, her face tilted up. "Just why *did* you bring me here, Jeremy?"

Chapter Three

Leah had her own ideas about why Jeremy had driven her to his house. Yes, he'd wanted to give her a break from the twins, but she also wondered if he was trying to convince her that there were advantages to marrying him. He obviously didn't want to talk about his wife or his marriage, and she could give him some space on that. Maybe eventually he'd tell her on his own. Still, she wanted to know what he was thinking.

She waited for his answer.

Looking almost like a boy who'd been caught with his hand in the cookie jar, he admitted, "I wanted you to see how comfortable you and the twins could be here."

Glancing around again at the beautiful furnishings, she didn't beat around the bush. "Pretty furniture in a beautiful house won't change my mind. I have to know in my heart that I'm doing the right thing."

"This wasn't meant to be some kind of bribe." His tone was as defensive as his stance.

"I know it wasn't, but it was meant to be a lure."

A tension-filled pause stretched between them, and he didn't deny it. Rather, he headed for the door, motioning her to follow. "Come on, I'll warm up some cider."

Although she followed him to the kitchen, he avoided her gaze. With quick economical movements, he heated the cider and filled two mugs, then they returned to the living room sofa and sat facing the fireplace.

After a few silent minutes while they sipped cider, Jeremy set down his mug and stared straight ahead into the leaping flames. "When my wife found out she was pregnant, we picked out the plans for this house. She was five months along when she was killed in a automobile accident."

Quickly, Leah set down her mug and touched his arm. "Jeremy, I'm sorry." He'd not only lost a wife, but a child, and her heart went out to him.

With his eyes still averted, he went on. "My life as I knew it crumbled. Since then I've worked, mostly, and spent very little time here."

Turning toward her then, he captured her hand. "But now we have twins. I want to hear their laughter echoing off of these walls. I want to see them playing outside. I want to watch them opening their presents on Christmas morning. I want to be a real father to them, not just see them for vacations once a year. And with all that, I want to get closer to you.''

The green of his eyes beckoned her to lean toward him, and after a few moments she did...instinctively...as if she belonged close to him. As he slipped his arm around her, she breathed in the scent of him, saw the yearning in his eyes and felt it in herself. His lips touched hers, and the fire between them burned away hesitation and doubts and thoughts of everything other than now. His tongue coaxed her lips apart, and she found herself wanting to get as close as she could get, wanting to know him in a meaningful way.

His tongue stroked her mouth, drawing a moan from her. As she slid her fingers into his hair, she loved the soft, springy feel of it. The passion that he'd drawn from her that night nine months ago bloomed and opened once more until she knew she was falling in love with this man...knew that he was much more than the father of her children. He was strong and caring, and over the past few days he'd shown her such tender kindness. Tears came to her eyes whenever she thought about it. Should she think about staying and living on the res? Should she consider marrying Jeremy?

But what about discovering where she truly belonged? What about her dreams? What about true love?

She believed him when he said he wanted to be a father to Brooke and Adam. But what kind of husband would he be? She *did* have deep feelings for him, but did Jeremy have feelings for her? Or did he simply want her to warm his bed? Her heart sinking, she considered the possibility that he merely wanted a replacement for the family he'd lost.

That thought broke through the haze of desire. That thought broke the hypnotic quality of his kiss. If she was only a replacement...

She stiffened and pulled away.

"What's wrong?" he asked, his breathing ragged.

Her pulse was still pounding and her skin tingled with the sensations that lingered, reminding her Jeremy wasn't only the father of her children, but a man she could love with all her heart.

She slid away from him to give both of them breathing space. "I think you should take me back to the res."

"Why?"

His gaze was probing and he wanted an honest answer. "Because kissing you confuses me."

He cocked his head and amusement twinkled in his eyes. "Maybe the confusion would go away if we kissed longer or more often."

She had to smile. "When I'm confused, I stop what I'm doing."

Taking her braid in his hand, he rubbed his thumb across the silky ends of her hair. "I think we'll have to change that strategy." Then he slipped his hand behind her neck, brought her toward him, and kissed her forehead. "Are you sure you want to leave?" he murmured.

It would be so easy to give in to this magnetic pull toward him, but she owed herself and her children and her mother much more than giving in to impulse or thinking about today rather than the future. "I need to go back to Laughing Horse, Jeremy."

Gazing down at her, he finally nodded. "I'll take you home."

Jeremy didn't seem angry as they drove back to the reservation, but he *did* seem distant. The twins had changed their lives, and she supposed he had as many thoughts to wrestle with as she did.

When they entered Leah's house, they could smell something cooking. Bessie was ladling soup into plastic containers. "You can freeze this," she said cheerfully. "Then you'll have it when you need it. Brooke's still sleeping and I gave Adam a bottle. They're both perfect angels. But you did get a phone call from Jenny McCallum. She wants you to call her back as soon as you get in."

Jeremy said, "I'll look in on Brooke and Adam."

By the time he returned to the kitchen, Leah was just hanging up the phone. "Jenny wants me to go to the Christmas Eve pageant tomorrow night at the elementary school."

"Does she know about the twins?" Jeremy asked.

"Bessie filled her in," Leah said with a smile. "I think she wants me there for moral support. She and Sara were supposed to sing a duet, and now obviously Sara can't. I think Jenny's scared to be performing on her own.''

''Would you like to go?'' Jeremy asked.

''I don't want to leave the twins again, but I feel as if I should be there for her.''

''We'll take the twins. Then you won't have to worry about them.''

''Oh, I don't know if we should. It will be cold.''

''We'll bundle them up,'' he assured her. ''I'll even put a blanket over them if that will make you feel better. I promise you, we can keep them warm and they'll be fine. You can feed Brooke when you need to and we'll take a bottle for Adam. They'll probably sleep through the whole thing.''

With a nod of her head, Bessie seconded his motion. ''Jeremy's right. It will do you good to go. You can't hibernate just because you're a new mother. After all, tomorrow night's Christmas Eve.''

Christmas Eve. One of the holiest nights of the year. She had already been blessed with a Christmas miracle. This season would always be special because of Brooke and Adam.

''I would like to go,'' Leah decided, giving in because she really did want to see Jenny perform.

Jeremy checked his watch. ''I have to go— rounds at the hospital.''

Walking him to the door, Leah said, ''Thank you for taking me out today. It was a nice break.''

He didn't say anything, just lifted her chin,

brushed his lips against hers, and then opened the door and left.

Later in the afternoon the clank of the mailbox lid closing alerted Leah to the mail's arrival. Bessie had gone home and the twins were napping. Leah opened the door, thinking about what she'd wear to the Christmas pageant…thinking about seeing Jeremy again. Reaching for the mail, she recognized Christmas cards among a few other envelopes. As she brought the stack inside, she noticed that one envelope was rather official-looking. She glanced at the return address—the Museum of History Through the Ages, Washington, D.C. It was one of the museums to which she'd sent her résumé.

Her heart raced as she went to the kitchen with the mail. Laying the stack on the counter, she opened the envelope and removed the letter, reading it quickly. The museum's personnel director had examined her résumé and background with interest and was requesting an interview! The letter stated the personnel office would be closed until after the New Year, but that Leah should call soon after to set up a date if she was still interested.

If she was still interested?

She had dreamed of this opportunity all of her life. *Of course* she was interested.

But then Leah thought of Jeremy and her growing feelings for him.

What was she going to do?

Strings of colorful paper chains, pictures children had drawn, as well as a tall Christmas tree decorated the school's all-purpose room where rows of folding chairs had been set up to face the stage. Leah sat with Adam cuddled in her arms, a bit nervous about being here with Jeremy, who was sitting next to her, holding Brooke, his arm comfortably brushing Leah's whenever he moved. In a town the size of Whitehorn, everyone knew everyone's business whether it was their concern or not. But on Christmas Eve with parents focused more on their children than on what was going on around them, she felt relatively unnoticed. Lynn Taylor, Jenny and Sara's teacher, had waved to her. Leah had had lunch with her and Jessica and Danielle a few times.

All the pageant-goers had their gazes trained on the stage where the narrator was recounting the Christmas story. As the angel chorus came on stage, Jeremy exchanged a smile with Leah. Jenny and Sara were wearing white robes, silver wings and gold halos.

Jeremy leaned close to Leah, his breath stirring the hair by her ear. "I can imagine Brooke and Adam up there."

When Leah turned to say she could imagine that, too, she found her face very close to Jeremy's. She could smell his cologne and thought he'd never looked more handsome then he did tonight in casual navy trousers and a blue cable-knit sweater. Thinking about the letter in her kitchen drawer, she faced forward again. She had until after the New Year to make her decision.

Giving her attention to the pageant, trying to temper her awareness of Jeremy's broad shoulders and his musky scent, she watched intently as Jenny stepped forward to sing a solo. Sara stood to the side of the angel chorus.

When Jenny glanced over her shoulder at Sara as if entreating her to come forward to sing with her, Sara just shook her head. Little Jenny suddenly looked petrified and stared at her mother and father who sat in the front row. Leah knew the five-year-old had rehearsed until the song was a part of her. They'd sung it together over and over again when Jenny had stayed on the reservation.

When the pianist played the first bars of the song, Jenny didn't begin. Her gaze met Leah's, as though she were pleading with Leah to do something for her. There was only one thing Leah knew to do. Standing, with Adam in her arms, she moved closer to the chorus and began to softly sing the words. As soon as the first few notes filled the air, Jenny sang with her. After the first line, Leah stopped and Jenny kept singing, filling the auditorium with her clear, young voice gathering strength the longer she sang. Leah slipped back into her seat as Jenny's voice rose high into the room and then ended to a burst of applause. The narrator continued with the story, and the wise men filed across the stage. When the curtain went down, the audience heartily applauded again.

The lights came on, and Lynn Taylor approached Leah. "Thank you so much for starting Jenny off. When I saw her panic, I forgot the words, too!"

"You have a beautiful voice," Jeremy said to Leah.

Leah felt her face flush with his compliment. "Thank you." When Adam wriggled in her arms, she rocked him gently. Leah kissed his forehead.

As Lynn gazed at the baby, there was longing in her expression. "What's his name?"

"Adam," Leah and Jeremy said in unison.

Ross Garrison, the attorney who handled Jenny McCallum's trust fund, joined the group. He and Lynn were engaged. Draping his arm around his fiancé's shoulders, he looked down at Adam tenderly. "I don't know if we're ready for this yet, but we *are* ready for the first step."

Lynn's blue eyes sparkled with mischief as she whispered to Jeremy and Leah, "Ross and I are eloping as soon as we leave here. We just have to say goodbye to the children, then we'll be on our way."

After Jeremy and Leah both congratulated them amid wishes for a merry Christmas, the couple headed for the stage.

Leah peeked inside Brooke's blanket to see if her little girl was still napping. She wasn't. Her dark eyes stared up at Jeremy as if she knew he was her father. Leah's heart ached as she thought of dreams and commitments and sacrifices and the decision she had to make.

A few minutes later, Jessica and Sterling McCallum descended the three steps from the stage and came toward Leah and Jeremy. "We want to thank you for helping Jenny as you did. We weren't sure what to do,'' Sterling said, his voice deep with gratitude.

Jessica smiled at Leah. ''Jenny told me your Cheyenne nickname is Little Bird Who Sings. Now I can see why.''

''When I was little, my mother told me I sang all the time. Now I usually just hum,'' Leah responded with a laugh.

Jessica looked from Leah to Jeremy, and Leah knew she didn't have to tell her friend that Jeremy was the twins' father. ''May I hold one of the babies?''

With a smile, Jeremy gave up Brooke. Jessica cooed over her for a few minutes, stroking the infant's hair, letting her finger trail down her cheek.

It wasn't long before Danielle approached them. ''The girls are talking with Lynn and Ross. At least Jenny is. Leah, she wants you to wait until she comes out here.''

''How is Sara doing?'' Leah asked gently.

''I had a specialist check her out again and there's nothing wrong with her physically. She just won't talk, and I'm worried that the men who kidnapped her will find out who she is somehow. She's the only one who can identify them.''

Sterling McCallum explained, ''Danielle and Sara will be staying with us over Christmas.''

With the added security at the ranch, Leah knew Sara and Danielle would be safe under Sterling's care. ''We'll pray that the men are caught soon so you don't have to worry,'' Leah assured Danielle.

Jenny and Sara came running down the steps

from the stage and stood in front of Leah and Jessica, eager to take a peek at the twins. Leah let them, then, after hugs all around, Jeremy helped Leah into her coat. Bundling the twins carefully, they carried them out to the Jeep.

On the drive back to the Laughing Horse Reservation, Brooke and Adam began fussing. By the time Jeremy parked, they were both proclaiming very loudly how hungry they were. Once inside the house Jeremy said, "I'll feed Adam. You see to Brooke."

"Yes, sir," Leah said with a mock salute.

Looking chagrined for a moment he said, "I guess I'm just used to taking charge."

Leah gave Jeremy a smile that said she understood as she took Brooke into the bedroom. Yet Jeremy's take-charge attitude was one of the reasons she had to be sure about any decision she made.

An hour later the twins had been changed and fed and were now sleeping in their cradles. Jeremy seemed to simply enjoy watching them, reminding Leah that there was something she'd been wanting to ask him since the twins had been born. Adam's Cheyenne features were obvious; Brooke's a little less so, though she'd have an exotic look that would probably turn heads. Leah wondered how Jeremy felt about their Native American heritage. "What do you see when you look at them, Jeremy?"

He seemed perplexed at her question. "I see my son and daughter."

"You don't see children who are part White, part

Northern Cheyenne and might not be accepted by either race?''

His gaze locked on hers. ''No. I see Brooke and Adam.''

Though Leah had suspected Jeremy held no prejudice, she felt relief at his assurance. The Indians on the res didn't accept outsiders easily. There had been talk about Jeremy Winters before he'd taken over for Kane at the clinic. But soon after his arrival, it was evident that Jeremy didn't see Cheyenne or White. He saw patients who needed his care. He treated everyone as equals.

Moving closer to her, Jeremy brushed a strand of Leah's hair from her cheek. ''And when I look at you, I see a beautiful woman with black hair and dark brown eyes who's smart and caring and the sexiest new mother I know.''

Her cheeks felt hot as she returned, ''And just how many new mothers do you know?''

He laughed and walked with her into the living room. ''It's late, and you need to get your sleep when the twins do.''

But at the door, neither of them reached for the knob. Jeremy looked down at Leah, and she could feel his gaze deep inside her. Sometimes she didn't know how to act when she was around him. Sometimes she was afraid for everything his presence could mean. But sometimes she had to stop thinking and just feel.

He seemed to drink her in, absolutely everything about her, and when he moved closer, she didn't pull away. His green eyes sparkled with desire, his chest rose and fell with the increased rate of his breathing, an increase she noted in hers, too. He reached out and took her long hair in his hands, letting it glide through his fingers. Then he held her face, slowly stroking her cheekbones with his thumbs.

"Oh, Leah," he murmured. He bent to her, and the magic of Christmas began.

There was longing in his kiss…and hunger. Leah recognized the hunger because she'd felt it once before, the night they'd made love. She'd given in to it then and she gave in to it now, because it was more powerful than she was, more potent than her dreams. As his tongue erotically brushed hers, her arms went around his neck.

His lips clung to hers, then he pulled away, and they gazed at each other. Leah felt dazed by the emotion and desire that had welled up inside of her. Jeremy Winters was a force to be reckoned with and she wished she knew what she should do about him.

Swallowing hard, she finally found her voice. "Would you like to come to dinner tomorrow? Bessie went shopping for me this afternoon and she and Joe will be here."

He gave her an off-kilter grin. "I thought I might have to eat my Christmas dinner at the hospital. I'd like very much to celebrate Christmas with you."

The lights in his eyes told her if she didn't open the door, another kiss could happen between them, another kiss that would confuse her more. So she reached for the knob and turned it.

He stepped outside, then asked, "What time tomorrow?"

"Around noon?"

"Noon it is. Merry Christmas, Leah."

"Merry Christmas, Jeremy."

As the moon shone down on him and he strode to his Jeep, Leah realized she wasn't *falling* in love with Jeremy Winters. She'd already fallen.

As Jeremy drove toward Whitehorn, the hum of his kiss with Leah still vibrated through his body. He wanted her in the same elemental way he had since the first day he'd met her. Somehow he had to prove to her that life here was better than life anywhere else. He thought of tomorrow, Christmas...having dinner with her. He'd already bought the twins a double stroller and a swing, but he could do so much more than that and surprise her. One of the department stores in the mall just on the edge of Whitehorn was supposed to be open till midnight. He was going to take advantage of that.

The next morning, as Jeremy showered and dressed, he couldn't help but hum Christmas carols. He even found himself at a church near the hospital, attending morning service. Ever since Gwen and their unborn child had died, Christmas had been merely a word. He'd spent Christmas Day in Oregon last year, but his father could care less about the holiday. His mother had established her own traditions with her husband and *his* children. Jeremy had gone through the motions when necessary, yet not felt any of the spirit, nor cared if he ever felt it again. But this year...

This year he had so much to celebrate.

When Leah opened the door to him, she was wearing an apron over her cream blouse and green wool skirt, and had never looked lovelier. Her hair was pulled back into a low ponytail tied with a red ribbon. All he wanted to do was to gather her in his arms and kiss her as he had last night, but before they even had time to exchange greetings, Bessie called from the kitchen. "Leah, where's your strainer? The gravy looks lumpy."

Leah smiled at him, her dark eyes sparkling. "Come on in. Joe is keeping watch over the twins. You can help him."

"I have a few things to get from the car," Jeremy said. "Then I'll be in."

As Jeremy carried in boxes and bags, Joe White-cloud said, "I think you bought out a store or two." The older man's black eyes danced with amusement. "But I can understand. You should have seen the stack of boxes we sent our son last week."

Jeremy knew that Bessie and Joe's son worked for a technology company on the west coast, and his work had kept him from coming home this Christmas. If Leah moved away, Jeremy might not see his children every holiday. He couldn't imagine being separated from them, especially on Christmas. "I can't wait until I can buy Adam baseball gear, and Brooke, well, whatever girls want at Christmas. I couldn't resist a few toys."

"A few?" Joe asked with a laugh.

When Leah came into the living room, her eyes grew wide. "Jeremy, what's all this?" Her gaze traveled over the stroller and swing, both with big red bows. He'd brought a stack of disposable diapers, two matching teddy bears, a big ball, a miniature truck, a doll and two mobiles. There was also a diaper bag with little animals running all over it, to replace the denim satchel Leah had carried to the pageant last night, which hadn't been big enough for all the baby paraphernalia she needed.

"Merry Christmas," Jeremy said with a huge grin.

But Leah wasn't smiling. As she went to the stroller and fingered the bow, as she took in everything he'd brought, her eyes became more troubled. "Jeremy, you shouldn't have done this."

"It's Christmas," he said with a shrug, as if that should explain it all. "If Brooke or Adam wake up while we're eating, we'll try the swing. I can always get a second one. The salesclerk said babies really like them, and the motion helps soothe them when they're fussy."

Leah glanced at the twins, who were sleeping in their cradles placed to the side of the armchair, and then back at Jeremy.

Obviously picking up the strained vibrations, Joe pushed himself up from the sofa. "I'll go see if I can help Bessie in the kitchen."

Leah moved a few steps closer to Jeremy. "I know you spent a lot of time choosing everything, and I don't want to seem unappreciative, but I can't accept all this."

"Why not?"

"Because it's too much!"

Jeremy had found such joy in picking out each item, in buying in abundance, in celebrating his fatherhood, that Leah's lack of enthusiasm made him defensive. "It's not too much. If I had known you were going to have twins, I would have bought more than this before now. They're basic things every child should have."

"Brooke and Adam don't need a stroller or a swing or toys they can't play with yet. All of this makes me feel as if I can't provide what they need."

"Can you?" Jeremy asked.

"*Need* means different things to different people. For now Brooke and Adam don't need much. They need my love and care, food and diapers. I can handle that."

His shoulders tensed. "What about six months from now, a year from now? Will you still be living on your savings?" He knew that's what she was probably doing. How else could she be managing? "I'm their father. I have the right to take care of them, too. I'm responsible for them as much as you are."

Taking a few steps back, Leah responded quickly. "I don't think this is about your being responsible for them. I think you're trying to convince me to stay, and presents won't do it."

He wanted to give Leah and the twins so much, everything he'd been denied giving Gwen and the child he'd lost. "You're making too big a deal out of this," he said curtly.

"Am I?" Leah asked, searching his face.

"These are Christmas presents. Period. Things I thought you could use and wouldn't buy for yourself. And if I want to buy my son and daughter toys that they can eventually play with, I don't see the harm in that. If you can't accept them, I'll keep them at my house until they grow into them." His tone was clipped and sounded hard without his meaning it to.

Leah touched his arm. "Jeremy..."

"Do you want to keep this stuff here or do you want me to pack it up in the Jeep?"

She looked up at him beseechingly. "Do you understand what I'm trying to say?"

"I understand that you think you're a single mother, and I guess you are. But I'm telling you that I have the means to buy my children whatever they need or want, and I'm going to do that, no matter what you say."

Leah's shoulders squared and her back became very straight. "I have to see to dinner. Just don't think I'm going to let you spoil them with material things when what they really need is so much more important than that." After another look at her sleeping infants, she went into the kitchen.

Jeremy wondered how a day that had started so right could have veered off track so swiftly, but no matter what Leah said, he would support his children the best way he knew.

Chapter Four

During Christmas dinner, Bessie and Joe kept the conversation moving. Bessie told Leah about the native crafts classes that would be held at the school on the res after the New Year, while Joe engaged Jeremy in a discussion of football. Leah hated the tension between her and Jeremy. It felt so wrong.

Maybe she should have simply accepted his presents graciously. But if she had accepted them without question, she would have felt indebted to him. She'd wanted to make it clear that she and the twins could make it on their own if they had to. Although she'd like to believe Jeremy was only thinking about Brooke and Adam, she had the feeling that he was trying to make up for something because of the wife and child he'd lost.

Bessie's pumpkin and cream cheese torte was a wonderful dessert, but Leah pushed half of hers away uneaten and so did Jeremy. As they sipped coffee, their gazes met over their cups and Leah yearned for Jeremy's love. Could she and the twins be more than a replacement for the family he'd lost?

Joe cleared his throat. "It seems like Adam and Brooke are going to give us a break."

"It's amazing how Adam settled down after we gave him that formula," Leah remarked after a quick glance at Jeremy. "He sleeps as soundly as Brooke does between feedings now."

"As well it should be," Bessie said with a smile. "They need their strength for growing up."

Jeremy leaned back in his chair. "That was a wonderful meal. Now I feel as if I need to work it off."

"Why don't you and Leah take a walk?" Bessie suggested. "The sun's shining."

"I really should help you clean up…" Leah began.

"No, you shouldn't," Bessie insisted. "Joe can help me. Go on, get your coat."

Leah had to admit she didn't know what to say to Jeremy and that's why she was hesitating. But a walk would feel good and they'd have a chance to iron things out.

After she made sure the twins were still sleeping soundly, Leah bundled up in her hooded parka, wrapped a scarf around her neck and slipped on mittens and boots. Jeremy's sheepskin jacket looked warm, but he turned up the collar and pulled on leather gloves. Then he opened the door for her and they stepped outside

"Are you sure you want me to come along?" Leah asked. "Bessie kind of put you on the spot."

"I don't mind, Leah." He looked annoyed at the question.

Paths had not been shoveled in front of some of the houses and they walked out in the street because it was easier. Coming to the end of one street, they turned onto another, their breath puffing out white in front of them. Leah could tell Jeremy was slowing his pace to hers. The sun shining on the snow had created an icy slush, and though Leah was careful, her foot slipped.

When Jeremy caught her by the elbow, his clasp was firm.

She said breathlessly, "Thank you."

Facing her, his gaze settled on her lips. "You're welcome."

The temperature outside seemed to shoot up, and she thought about his last kiss, about how he'd felt and tasted. She'd never considered herself a sensual woman until she'd met Jeremy. Now everything about him titillated her senses.

With a bolstering breath, she began walking again.

They passed small square houses, one looking very much like the next, some decorated for Christmas, some not. Life on the res was still a struggle. From what she'd heard and seen, it wasn't as bad as it had been years ago when her mother had taken her away. There were good people trying to change things for the better. Jackson Hawk for one. His law office was located in the Tribal Council building. His wife, Maggie, who had once been an agent for the government, assisted him. Then there was Sam Brightwater, a contractor, who'd been instrumental in the building of a new elementary school wing here on Laughing Horse. Jessica McCallum's social welfare expertise helped the Tribal Council decide on programs for teenagers and adults. There was goodness here, and the Cheyennes' support of their extended families and their community life was tight-knit and enduring.

Leah could feel her ties to her mother strongly here. And though she'd been a part of this life for the past twenty months, she still didn't feel as if she really belonged. Her mother's dream for her had always been so real, so specific, so far-reaching.

A church steeple rose up into the blue sky as they walked, and Leah was drawn toward it as if her mother were calling her there. She turned to Jeremy. "I'd like to stop at the church. Do you want to come in with me?"

He looked down at her with green eyes that didn't give a hint as to what he was feeling. "Sure," he said.

"Do you attend church?" she asked him as they slowly mounted the steps.

"I did this morning."

When she stopped to question the message underlying his words, he stopped, too. "I was angry after I lost Gwen. God was the last person I wanted to talk to.''

"And now?" Leah asked softly.

"Let's just say I'm opening the lines of communication again. How about you?"

"I rarely miss a Sunday. Mom always taught me to be grateful for blessings. Going to church just helps me remember what my blessings are.''

They continued up the steps and Jeremy opened the wooden door for her.

The church wasn't large, nor was it elaborate, but Leah always felt a sense of peace here. The pews were wooden and worn, the pulpit a simple lectern. But there was an Advent wreath on a table, and pine boughs, evergreen wreaths and red bows everywhere. Two small stained-glass windows, one on either side of the altar, splayed color across the creche, and Leah stepped forward, drawn by the nativity scene displayed there.

Leah stood looking at the figures, thinking of her own babies. Tears welled up and rolled down her cheeks.

Jeremy watched her. "Leah?" he asked, concern in his voice.

"I just wish my mom were here to meet her grandchildren.''

When his arm went around her, it seemed so natural to lean against him. They stood there like that for a very long time, unaware of the minutes ticking by, unaware of everything but each other and the scene in front of them.

Leah's tears had dried by the time she looked up at him again. "Maybe we should go?"

He nodded. But as they passed the last pew, Jeremy took her arm and said, "Wait a minute."

After she stopped, he admitted, "I understand that you don't want me to shower Brooke and Adam with unnecessary gifts, but *you* have to understand that I need to feel as if I'm making a difference in their lives."

"I know," Leah responded. "I'm sorry I reacted as I did. I *am* grateful for everything you've done. That whole carload of presents was just a bit... overwhelming."

"That's the way I feel sometimes when I look at the twins," he confessed.

"Me, too."

His smile spread to his eyes. "Let's go back and see if they're awake yet."

As Jeremy opened the door, Leah realized her love for him was growing stronger each day. But how did he feel about her, and how did he fit into her future?

As Leah changed the twins, fed them and bathed them on the day after Christmas, she thought about Jeremy. They'd returned from their walk yesterday and cared for Brooke and Adam, played with them a little by holding them and talking to them, while Bessie and Joe looked on like proud grandparents. Afterward, the four of them had played a board game. Jeremy's gaze had met Leah's often, their fingers had touched, their elbows grazing now and then. But as early evening had approached, Jeremy left to look in on patients at the hospital. With no moment alone, he hadn't kissed her before he'd gone, and Leah had felt strangely sorry about that.

With the twins napping, Leah went to the porch for her morning paper. As she brought it inside she glanced at the front page headline—Kidnapping Gone Awry. With growing dismay, Leah read the article.

The reporter wrote how Sara Mitchell had been mistakenly kidnapped instead of Jennifer Mc-Callum. He went on to say how Sara was probably the only one who could describe the two men who had worn ski masks when they'd kidnapped her, how Dr. Jeremy Winters had found the little girl walking alongside of the road on December eighteenth, how the holly berries that had been in her hair were peculiar to a specific area outside of Whitehorn, leading the police to a cave where the kidnappers had most likely kept her.

Since deputy sheriff Shane McBride was out of town on his honeymoon, Sterling McCallum, a special investigator, had been assigned to the case and had found one of Sara's hair ribbons not far from the cave. But there had been no further evidence leading to the kidnappers, and only Sara held the secret as to who they were. And for some unknown reason, trauma-induced or otherwise, Sara couldn't talk.

A chill skipped up Leah's spine. Little Sara could be in even more danger with all of this information made public. The kidnappers now even knew her name. Leah bet Danielle was probably going crazy with worry. Hurrying to the phone, remembering Danielle and Sara had spent Christmas with the McCallums, she dialed the McCallums' number. The answering machine came on. She decided not to leave a message, but to try again later.

Late morning on the day after Christmas, Jeremy closed the door to his lawyer's office and crossed the reception area to the outside entrance. Yesterday had unsettled him, giving him a taste of what he'd always wanted—a wife, children, and an extended family to spend holidays with. He had to convince Leah to want it, too. But she threw him off balance...she always had. When he'd first met her, he'd thought she was quiet and shy. She might be quiet sometimes, but she wasn't shy, and she had a way of being assertive that told him in no uncertain terms that she was an independent woman and wouldn't be dictated to by a man. The most confusing part of all was that he liked her that way. Gwen hadn't been assertive *or* independent. She'd always let him take the lead; she'd always stepped back in his shadow. Leah, on the other hand, walked beside him.

In the middle of the night last night, Jeremy had awakened thinking about Brooke and Adam, and he'd known exactly what he was going to do—set up a trust fund for each of them. That way he'd feel as if he were securing their future. Leah couldn't possibly object to that, could she? Teresa Nighthawk had done everything she could to secure

Leah's future. That's why Leah was having so much difficulty letting go of an old dream and replacing it with a new one. Besides giving his children security, he wanted to give Brooke and Adam the freedom to do whatever they wanted with their lives. No matter what Leah said, he was going to do that.

When he stepped outside his lawyer's office, a chilling breeze blew across him and he snapped his sheepskin jacket closed. Turning in the direction of his Jeep parked on the street beyond the Whitehorn sheriff's building, he saw Danielle Mitchell standing in front of the office, her auburn hair flying around her face in a blast of wind.

He'd met Danielle and her husband Kyle after he'd moved to Whitehorn and opened his practice. They'd attended charity functions the hospital sponsored. When he'd brought Sara home after she'd escaped the kidnappers, he'd examined her and reassured Danielle over and over that with love and attention, her daughter would recover from the trauma of being kidnapped.

But right now Danielle looked almost as upset as she had after her husband, Kyle, an FBI agent, had disappeared mysteriously two years ago. As Jeremy got closer, he noticed she was wiping a tear from her cheek. "Danielle, what's wrong? Has something happened to Sara?"

She shook her head and turned up the collar of her long, black coat. "Did you see the article in the *Whitehorn Journal* this morning?" she asked him.

He'd brought in the paper but never looked at it.

He'd been too intent on making an appointment with his lawyer. "No, I haven't. What was in it?"

"Some reporter was stupid enough to print everything he could find out about Sara and the kidnapping, and reminded the kidnappers that Sara's the only one who can identify them. Now they know her name! I asked Sterling to call a man Kyle knew at the FBI. Luke Mason says he'll look into protection for her. In the meantime Sterling insists we stay with him and Jessica. I know he's doing everything he can, but I'm so afraid for Sara. We can't stay with the McCallums indefinitely."

Her voice quivered and Jeremy felt sorry for her. Without Kyle by her side, she had the burden of this situation with Sara. "Do you want to go have a cup of coffee?"

She hesitated a moment, but then responded, "I'd like that. If you're sure you have time."

"I don't have office hours until one. Do you want to go to the Hip Hop?"

She nodded.

Soup was heating on the stove when Leah tried to call the McCallums again. She hadn't reached anyone there all day and it was almost five o'clock. The phone rang a few times, but then Jessica answered.

"Hi, Jessica, it's Leah. I saw the article in the paper today and was worried about Danielle and Sara."

"I couldn't believe it when I saw it," Jessica said, her anger evident. "Danielle is terribly upset.

I convinced her and Sara to stay with us for a few more days. Sterling's hoping that either something will break soon or Sara will start talking. I took the girls sledding this morning, then when Danielle came home, we went to a movie. We're trying not to let Sara and Jenny see how worried we are. Hold on a minute and I'll get Danielle.''

In a few moments Danielle came to the phone. ''Hi, Leah.'' Her voice sounded as if she were purposely trying to be cheerful.

''How are you holding up?'' Leah asked.

''Not as well as I'd like, but I'm determined to keep Sara safe whether the FBI protects her or not.'' She told Leah that Sterling had called Luke Mason. ''It's just that on top of everything else, a few weeks ago I sent—''

Leah waited as Danielle gathered her emotions once more.

''I sent Kyle a letter in care of the FBI. I don't know if he's alive or dead, but if he's alive, I've got to put some order back in my life and Sara's.''

Not pressing her friend for more, Leah knew Danielle would talk if she needed to. ''It's good you have Jessica and Sterling.''

''*And* you and Jeremy. I ran into him when he was coming out of Gil Brown's office. He offered to buy me a cup of coffee and helped me settle down enough so that I didn't come back here looking as worried as I felt.''

''Gil Brown?'' Leah knew he was a lawyer whose office was located practically next door to the sheriff's office. Why was Jeremy seeing a lawyer? "Did Jeremy say why he was seeing Mr. Brown?"

"No, he didn't. I was so wrapped up in talking about Sara, I didn't let the him get a word in edgewise."

Covering a ripple of worry that washed through her, Leah said casually, "Jeremy's a good listener."

After Leah spoke with Danielle a few more minutes, telling her to call if there was anything she could do, she hung up. But her mind was racing. Why had Jeremy seen Gil Brown? Did it have something to do with yesterday and her reaction? Was he trying to find out what his rights were? To see if he could make her stay in Whitehorn? To take the children away from her if she didn't stay?

After all, he was well respected in this community—a doctor—and he had plenty of money. She, on the other hand, didn't even have a viable job at the moment. But she did have that offer for an interview. If Jeremy did anything, anything at all, to try to take her children from her, she'd fight like she'd never fought before.

The rest of the day passed slowly as Leah talked and sang to the twins, fed them, played with their fingers and toes, rocked them and loved them. All the while her mind was on Jeremy's visit to the lawyer. She didn't have the money to hire an attorney. If he wanted to take Brooke and Adam away from her, what could she do except run?

Away from the man she loved?

If he was planning a strategy with a lawyer, he couldn't possibly have feelings for her.

There was only one thing she could do—confront him about it, try to catch him by surprise so she could learn what he was planning. She couldn't believe how deep the hurt went when she thought about it, how very much she'd come to care about him…to love him. But one-sided love wasn't enough…never enough to make a marriage succeed.

She'd never known much about marriage, never seen it working until she'd come back to the res with her mother. There were successful marriages all around her. Sterling and Jessica had been through so much together and had held fast. Then there was Bessie and Joe, Sam Brightwater and Julia, with their new baby, Jackson and Maggie, Kane and his wife Moriah. All of these couples had been through fire of one sort or another and had come out strong, loving each other in a way any passerby could see. That's the kind of marriage Leah wanted—the kind of marriage that lasted forever.

Every day since the twins had been born, Jeremy had either called or stopped in. Each minute ticked by on an inner clock as Leah waited, wondered and worried. Because of the holiday, he had office hours this afternoon and then he'd have evening rounds at the hospital.

After Brooke and Adam were settled for the evening, Leah wished she could concentrate on something, anything but the questions that grew bigger and bolder with each passing hour. Finally she settled down at the kitchen table with a vest she was beading. Her mother had taught her the craft years before, but Leah had only taken it up again since she'd been back on the res. It was a black velvet vest and she was beading it in white and shades of blue. It was almost finished, but even her intense concentration couldn't put her fears to rest, and she finally turned on the radio to have something to distract her.

She recognized the sound of Jeremy's Jeep as he pulled up outside. Then she heard the door closing and, finally, his boots on the porch. Taking a few calming breaths, she anticipated his knock and eventually it came. Carefully laying the vest on the table, she went to answer the door.

He was smiling. "Sorry I'm so late." He held up a bag in his hand. "I stopped at the Hip Hop and asked Janie to box up tonight's special. I don't even know what it is, but I can share it with you if you'd like."

Her stomach was tied in knots. "I've already eaten."

Coming inside, he dropped the bag on the coffee table and snapped open his coat, shrugged it off, and laid it on the back of the chair. "Did Brooke and Adam have a fussy spell tonight?"

"For about an hour, then they settled down fairly easily. Jeremy…"

He sat on the sofa and was ready to open up the bag when he looked at her. "Is something wrong?"

Her hands were sweaty and she stuck them into the pockets of her denim skirt for a moment. He was acting so normal, as if this were any other night. But what she knew or thought she knew wouldn't let her treat it that way. She couldn't make casual conversation as if nothing had changed. "I spoke with Danielle earlier."

"Oh…the article in the *Journal*. I wish that reporter would lose his job, but the bottom line is, the story probably sold a lot of papers. I guess she told you we had coffee together. I haven't seen her this unhinged since…well, since Kyle disappeared."

There was only one way to do this and that was to jump right into it. "Danielle told me she saw you coming out of Gil Brown's office."

Jeremy took a plastic container out of the bag. "Yes, she did."

"Why were you there?" Leah asked.

His hands stilled on the box. "Why do you think I was there?"

"I don't know. I can only guess one reason. Were you looking into what your rights are? Do you plan to take the twins away from me?" She had to know exactly what was on his mind, and the only way to do that was to lay her worst fear out there for him to see.

But instead of giving her an answer, he stood. "That's what you've been thinking? That I stopped at Brown's office to look into taking Brooke and Adam away from you?"

There was a mixture of anger and incredulity in his tone that confused her. "If I won't let you give them everything you want, if I do plan on moving away—''

"For God's sake, don't you know me at all?" His voice was deep and angry.

"I thought I did, but when Danielle told me, I couldn't help thinking—''

Again he cut her off. "Damn it, Leah! No, I don't want you to leave. Yes, I want to be a father to my children. Sure, I want to give them everything I can give them—and that *is* why I was at Gil Brown's office.''

Her heart started beating so rapidly she could hardly catch her breath. "Then you *are* planning something.''

"Yes, I'm planning something.'' His voice went very low but was so vehement she could practically feel the vibration of it. "I instructed Brown to set up trust funds for Brooke and Adam.''

It took almost a minute for his words to sink in. "Trust funds?''

"Yes, trust funds. For college, for trips abroad, for trade school, for whatever Brooke and Adam are going to need in their lives.''

"Oh, Jeremy,'' she said softly, her voice quivering as guilt for her doubts overtook her.

"How could you possibly think I would connive to take them away from you?''

"You seem to love them as much as I do.'' It was the only excuse she could think of.

"I don't *seem* to. I *do* love them as much as you do, and that's why I would never take them away from you. They need you, probably more than they could ever need me. Don't you think I know that?" He sounded furious and frustrated and altogether disgusted with her.

"I don't know what to say."

He stared at her for a few moments. "You obviously don't know how to trust, either." Picking up his jacket from the chair, he headed for the bedroom. After he looked in on Brooke and Adam, he crossed to the door. "I thought we at least had basic trust between us, Leah, but I guess I was wrong." He nodded to the coffee table. "Toss that out if you don't want it. I've lost my appetite."

Before she could even think of a way to apologize to him, he'd left and closed the door behind him.

She stared at the plastic container, then sank into the armchair, her chest tight, tears only a blink away. What could she do to make this up to him? How could she ever convince him to give her another chance to trust him?

Oh, Mom, she prayed, *just what do I do now?*

Chapter Five

After being up with both twins at three in the morning and then again at six, Leah dozed off once she got them settled again. Brooke awakened her at ten, and it was too late to get ready for church. She went about their usual morning routine, thinking all the while about Jeremy. And she kept thinking about him throughout the day until that evening when he called. His voice was cool and polite as he inquired about the twins, and Leah felt as if he didn't really want to talk to her.

She needed to apologize to him, but she couldn't do it over the phone, not when he was putting up such a wall between them. She had an appointment with George McGruder in the morning to check the twins' weight and make sure everything was okay in the absence of the pediatrician who had first seen them. Leah knew Dr. McGruder's office was in the same complex as Jeremy's. Maybe afterward she would stop by and see Jeremy and tell him how very sorry she was for doubting him.

Bessie offered to drive Leah and the babies on Monday morning, insisting she had errands she could run while Leah and the twins were with the doctor. It was as if Bessie was determined to take Teresa Nighthawk's place in Leah's life, and Leah was grateful.

Dr. McGruder pronounced both babies happy, healthy and growing. Afterward, Leah put the twins in a double carrier made of soft leather that fit across her chest so she could keep the babies close to her. They could feel the warmth of her body and seemed content. As she picked up the diaper bag and walked down the hall toward Jeremy's suite of offices, she was anxious about seeing him. Her mouth went dry as she opened the door into his waiting room.

Once inside, Leah looked around with dismay. There were four patients waiting, and Leah knew Jeremy would be too busy to see her now. As she was about to turn to leave, a nurse opened the door that lead to the examining rooms and spotted her.

Mary Jansen, a woman in her fifties, smiled at Leah as she called the next patient inside. The man passed through the door and Mary called out, "Second door on the right," before she turned her attention back to Leah. "Would you like to see Dr. Winters?"

Mary had helped Jeremy at the clinic on the res. "I don't want to bother him if he's busy," Leah said. She also didn't want to have a rushed conversation with him, and they couldn't do more than that with this many people waiting.

"Are the babies sleeping?" Mary asked, sounding hopeful that they weren't. The look in her eyes said Jeremy must have told her about the twins or she'd heard about them via the Whitehorn grapevine.

Leah crossed to her, knowing Mary was a kind woman, hoping she wouldn't judge.

With a tender expression, Mary looked down at the twins. "Which is Brooke and which is Adam?"

Leah had dressed Brooke in a green terry jumpsuit and Adam in a yellow one. After she introduced Mary to both of them, the nurse cooed over the infants. Then she commented, "It's so great Jeremy has somebody to care about again. When his wife and child died, he was devastated. Now all he talks about are Brooke and Adam."

There was no doubt that the twins meant a lot to Jeremy. But one question still plagued Leah. Were she and the babies simply replacements for the wife and unborn child that he had lost? Did she mean anything to him separate from their twins? She knew this wasn't the place to talk to Jeremy. She needed to be alone with him, to apologize and to have her questions answered. Making an excuse to Mary, she quickly left the office.

That evening, Leah was washing her supper dishes when there was a knock on the door. She quickly dried her hands, went to the door and opened it.

Jeremy stood there, his expression neutral, his gaze unreadable.

"Come in," she said, stepping back.

After he crossed the threshold, he took off his gloves and stuffed them into his jacket pocket. "Mary told me you came to the office this morning. Why did you leave without seeing me?"

Suddenly faced with Jeremy in person, Leah couldn't remember anything she'd wanted to say. "I had an appointment with Dr. McGruder and thought I'd stop in. But your waiting room was full and I—I was afraid the babies would get too fussy."

Unsnapping his jacket, Jeremy shrugged it off and tossed it over the arm of a chair. "And why did you stop in?"

He was standing in front of her, dressed in suit trousers and a white shirt with the sleeves rolled up. His tie was slightly askew, and she longed for the freedom to tug it off altogether. Being a new mother hadn't dimmed her attraction to him one iota. "I came to ask you to forgive me for doubting you. I'm sorry, Jeremy."

At first she didn't think he was going to accept her apology, but then some of the rigidity went out of his stance.

"I would *never* try to take the twins away from you. I came from a divorced household, spending part of the year with my mother, part of it with my father. It was unsettling, unstable, and difficult to create bonds that lasted, especially with other children. I wouldn't do that to my son and daughter. They need a stable base with you, Leah. But I intend to be just as much a part of their lives.''

''But if I move away—''

''*Are* you going to move away?''

She thought about the letter in the kitchen drawer. Should she tell Jeremy about it? Not now. Not yet. Maybe not at all. But she had to be honest with him. ''I don't know.''

Reaching out and taking her hand, he pulled her with him over to the sofa. As they sat, their shoulders and hips brushed, and neither of them moved away.

Keeping her hand in his, Jeremy laced his fingers with hers. ''Are Brooke and Adam sleeping?''

She nodded, gazing into his green eyes, wanting him in a way that went beyond their bond of parenthood.

''Everything has happened very fast between us, but I want you to trust me, Leah.''

''Trusting takes time.''

''I know.'' Bending close to her, he murmured, ''And maybe it takes a little persuasion, too.''

When he brushed his lips back and forth across hers, need rose up, and she realized how very little persuading he'd have to do for her to give him her whole heart, maybe everything she was. He released her hand and touched her face, then his tongue teased her lips. As they parted, he took full advantage.

Jeremy tasted hot and dark and forbidden, but Leah knew she'd fallen in love with much more than his sex appeal. She'd fallen in love with *him*.

As wind howled outside, emphasizing the silence within, Jeremy's kisses became longer and deeper. Their bodies strained toward each other. Leah could tell Jeremy wanted her, and she wanted him. But she also knew she couldn't go any farther and didn't want to lead him on.

Pushing away from him, she murmured, "We should stop. It's too soon..."

Caressing her cheek, he looked down at her. "I know it's too soon. I just want to kiss you and touch you and hold you."

She saw the deep tenderness in his eyes and realized he meant it. "I want to kiss and touch and hold you, too."

Groaning, he kissed her again with a fierce hunger. His hand slipped beneath the hem of the loose sweater she wore with her skirt and paused on her midriff.

His touch was an erotic match to her already smoldering need. Feeling freer than she'd felt in a long time with him, she tugged open his tie and kissed him back, trying to show him her love. Her fingers fumbled with his shirt buttons until finally she felt his hot skin. His chest hair was springy and soft, and she remembered another night and how their babies were conceived.

Jeremy's desire for Leah was so ferocious it seemed to have a life of its own. He'd been furious with her when she'd accused him of seeing a lawyer for custody reasons. But this morning, after Mary had told him that Leah had stopped in, he'd realized the anger had come from something else. Her distrust had made him feel unbearably alone. She and the twins were becoming his world, and he couldn't imagine his life without them.

He didn't *want* to imagine his life without them. Now he tried to tell her that with each sweep of his tongue and the depths of his kisses. Knowing he was stoking a need he couldn't satisfy, at least for a few more weeks, he thought about stopping. But Leah and the moment became more important than satisfaction. Somehow he had to convince her she needed him. He had to convince her to stay.

There was only one way to do that—make her want him as much as he wanted her. As a new mother, what had given her pleasure before, might not now. Yet being creative was part of the adventure and the challenge. Slowly, he stroked the skin below her breasts. She softly moaned, and passion shimmered between them.

Breaking the kiss, he rained kisses down Leah's neck under her luxurious hair. The way she said his name told him of the deep yearning she felt, too. When he rubbed his cheek against her hair, he breathed in orange blossoms and Leah and the scent of baby lotion, which seemed ever-present in the house now. Her hands, as soft as velvet and twice as arousing, slid down his chest, and he forgot time and place and reason.

His mouth sealed to hers again, and soon he'd tossed the pillows from the back of the sofa to the floor and lay facing her. Being this close was sweet torture. As he stroked her hair, she worked his shirt from his trousers, and when her hands caressed his ribs, he shuddered.

Pushing her hair back, he kissed under her ear. "I don't want to hurt you," he murmured, grateful that she could find pleasure in what they were doing so soon after the birth of their babies.

"You're not," she assured him as she explored his chest again.

This time when he reached under her sweater, he didn't hesitate. He touched the skin on her side, making slow circles that brought soft sounds from her throat. Wanting desperately to touch her breasts, knowing it was best not to, he instead smoothed her skirt up her slender leg, letting his hand leave a trail of teasing seduction. Her skin was so soft, so silky, so perfect. As his hand dallied on her thigh, her breaths became short and shallow.

"Oh, Jeremy, it feels so good. I just wish I could—"

"So do I," he said, his voice husky. He stroked her, letting his hand slide back to her knee.

When she shifted slightly, he wondered if he should stop.

But then her knee slid between his thighs, giving him pleasure. He thought fleetingly about stopping her. Instead, he kissed her again, taking whatever she could give him. He'd dreamed of her kisses; he'd dreamed of their bodies touching; he'd dreamed of creating magic between them again.

Caught up in the pleasure she was giving him,

he stroked her tongue until Leah brought her hand to him and caressed him through his trousers and underwear.

He tore his mouth from hers. "Leah, stop! You can't—"

"Why not?" Her voice was innocent in its softness.

"Because I can't give you the same kind of satisfaction. It wouldn't be fair."

"You *are* satisfying me. I just want to show you..." When she trailed off and passed her hand down the length of him again, he didn't think about pressing her for what she'd been about to say.

It had been forever since he'd touched her and she'd touched him so intimately. He was still thinking about stopping her, still thinking about giving her more pleasure when suddenly his restraint broke under the gentle touch of her hand, under the sensuality of lying here with a woman he'd wanted more than he'd ever wanted anyone, especially now that she was the mother of his children. Lost in the power of Leah's touch, he let her pleasure him until her tender stroking took him beyond the breaking point. His climax rocked him, making him shudder, making him wish Leah could experience it, too.

Even though he was a doctor, even though he'd been married, even though he'd had his share of experience with women, when his breathing returned to normal, he was embarrassed. "I shouldn't have let you do that," he murmured.

"Just consider it my belated Christmas gift to you."

He saw the smile in her eyes, the lingering sparkles of pleasure that satisfying him had given to her. He kissed her then, sweetly and softly until a baby's cry broke the silence.

"It's Brooke," Leah murmured.

"I know. Her cry is so different from Adam's." They gazed at each other, sharing the bond of recognition.

"I have to go to her," Leah said.

"Before you do, I want to ask you something. Will you go out with me on New Year's Eve? There's a bash at the Hip Hop, and I'd like for us to go together…as a couple. We don't have to stay long."

"I'd like that," she said with a wide smile. "I'll check with Bessie to see if she can baby-sit and let you know."

Jeremy couldn't keep himself from kissing Leah again, from trying to show her what she meant to his life.

Dressing for New Year's Eve, Leah wondered what Jeremy would think of her soft white blouse and beaded vest, her black velvet skirt and high heels. After assessing her hair, she decided to pull some of it to the top of her head and braid it. Using black velvet ribbon, she tied one piece at her crown and the other at the end of the braid. When she heard a male voice in the living room talking to Bessie, she knew Jeremy had arrived.

There was no doubt she was nervous about tonight. She and Jeremy seemed to be getting closer and closer. Though, since that night on the couch, his kisses had been less incendiary and more chaste. The past two nights, besides spending time with the twins, they'd also talked. He'd told her more about his childhood and his parents' divorce; she'd shared stories with him about growing up in Chicago and how her heritage had sometimes set her apart, but how she'd made a few good friends whose loyalty and caring were still important to her even though they were miles away. She was disappointed that Jeremy hadn't talked more about his marriage or his wife, yet she hadn't brought it up. When he was ready to tell her, he would.

As Leah stepped through the doorway into the living room, Jeremy's gaze locked to hers. "You look fantastic."

"So do you," she responded, admiring the fine cut of his navy pin-striped suit, his pristine white shirt, the navy and red silk tie. He was so handsome, her heart raced.

Bringing one hand from behind his back, he said, "I brought this for you."

The sight of the beautiful red roses and white baby's breath arranged as a wrist corsage warmed her inside. "How lovely!" She bowed her head to smell the flowers. The fragrance of the flowers was as heady as her desire to touch Jeremy and have him kiss her again. Although she was wearing heels, she still had to stand on tiptoe to kiss his cheek. "Thank you."

The lights in Jeremy's eyes told her he wanted much more than a token kiss. But as his arm curved around her waist to pull her close to him again, Bessie called to them from the sofa. "You two have fun tonight."

Jeremy's hand settled familiarly on Leah's hip and he responded, "You can count on it."

The Hip Hop Café was essential to Whitehorn's community life. Not only did it serve great specials at reasonable prices, but it was a meeting place, a roundtable, the spot where Whitehorn's grapevine started and stopped. One of Whitehorn's chief suppliers of gossip was Lily Mae Wheeler. She knew everything there was to know about everybody. Leah and Jeremy passed her as they stepped inside the café with its shiny bright New Year's Eve decorations and spirited conversation. Coming here tonight as Jeremy's date wouldn't go unnoticed. But Jeremy seemed oblivious to the arched brows and curious looks as he found them a booth, helped Leah take off her coat and slip on her corsage.

"It looks different tonight," Leah remarked, noticing the strobe lights near the jukebox, the red and silver streamers, the platters of sandwiches and snacks sitting on the counter.

"So do you," Jeremy said in a low husky voice.

Suddenly everything in the café disappeared, except for Jeremy. He took her hand across the table and wrapped her fingers into his palms.

"People are going to talk," she said, blushing.

"Does it matter?" he asked as he glanced around. He did see some people watching.

Instead of answering, she returned the question. "Does it matter to you?"

"I don't care what people say, Leah. My life is mine to live. Now you and the twins are in it. I'm not going to hide how I feel about that."

She wished he'd tell her exactly how he *did* feel...about her. But that wasn't the kind of conversation to have in the midst of a crowd.

Someone started the jukebox. The music was slow and sentimental and Jeremy squeezed her hand as he smiled at her. "Would you like to dance?"

Tonight she'd like to do anything that brought her closer to Jeremy. She nodded. As they walked to the space around the jukebox, Leah saw Kane Hunter take his wife Moriah into his arms. Sam Brightwater and his wife Julia also began dancing and smiled at Leah when they saw her. There was another couple Leah recognized—Wayne Kincaid, little Jennifer McCallum's half brother, and his wife, Carey. But as Jeremy took Leah into his arms, everyone else faded away.

Jeremy's arm around her felt protective as his hand settled gently in the small of her back. His other hand engulfed hers as he brought it to his chest. "For safekeeping," he teased.

The fabric of his suit coat was roughly sensual against her hand. His cologne was musky, and she loved the scent of it. She loved the scent of him. He guided her in small steps that weren't taxing, but rather swayed into the music. It was easy dancing with him, easy being close to him, easy to want so much more than a dance. They gazed at each other, lost in a magic world of lights and streamers and new chances.

Jeremy bent his head, and his lips trailed by her temple, sending quivers of excitement through her. "I'd rather be someplace alone with you," he murmured.

"But New Year's Eve is for celebrating," she teased.

Leaning slightly away, he searched her face. "I think the two of us celebrating the night alone could be very...exciting."

She remembered the other night on the sofa, the delicious sensations of having Jeremy touch her, his arousing kisses. She might not be able to make love with him for a few weeks or so, but she could certainly enjoy everything else. All of it felt so right with Jeremy.

So what about that interview offer? a little voice in her head asked.

She could tell Jeremy about it, but she didn't want to spoil this wonderful night. Maybe she could find a sense of belonging with Jeremy. Although her mother had enabled her to get a degree and pursue a career anywhere she wanted, wasn't happiness the ultimate success? Could a job in Washington, D.C., make her any happier than being here with Jeremy?

They were questions that might take a little time to answer. Or maybe not even time, but just the right words from Jeremy. As one song led into another, she knew that this man could be her home and her future if he felt the same way about her that she felt about him.

"We'll be alone tonight after Bessie leaves." She knew her words invited him to stay...she knew tonight could change her life.

"Do you know what I'd like?" he asked.

"What?"

"To fall asleep with you in my arms."

The idea that he simply wanted to hold her, to be close to her as she wanted to be close to him, brought tears to her eyes. "I'd like that, too."

Jeremy pressed her to him and rubbed his jaw in her hair.

When the song ended, they stopped dancing, but Jeremy didn't release her. Absorbed in each other, they couldn't seem to break apart until Carey Kincaid came up to them. Jeremy introduced Leah to Carey, explaining she was also a doctor.

"I know," Leah responded. "You and Kane Hunter share office space, right?"

Carey smiled. "We sure do." Addressing Jeremy, she said, "We missed you at the Christmas dinner last week."

"Something came up," he answered easily.

"Something like twins?" Carey asked with a smile. "You know, don't you, that rumors are running rampant? In a community like Whitehorn, the gossip starts with the whisper of the wind."

"Are you asking me if it's true, Carey?" he teased his colleague.

Carey blushed but responded, "I could help nix it if it's not."

With his arm still around Leah, he leaned close to Carey and murmured loud enough for Leah to hear, too, "It's true. I'm the proud father of a boy and a girl. And Leah's the proud mother."

Carey extended her hand to him and then to Leah. "Congratulations."

Leah felt that Carey Kincaid was sincerely happy for them.

After speaking with them for a few more minutes, Carey said, "I'd better find my husband before he sends out a search party. And Jeremy, I *am* really happy for you. I know how much this means to you."

The message beneath Carey's words was clear— *I know you lost a child and I'm sorry for that, but I'm rejoicing with you now that you're a father.*

Again Leah wondered if she and the twins were simply filling a hole in Jeremy's life, or if they meant a lot more.

Jeremy guided Leah to the trays of food on the counter. They sipped sherbert punch, ate sandwiches and guacamole dip and Christmas cookies. Every now and then they became involved in a conversation with someone they knew from Whitehorn. But most of the time, they talked with each other and did nothing to restrain the electricity that sizzled between them.

They were dancing again when a woman tapped Jeremy on the shoulder. "May I cut in?" she asked pleasantly.

With interest, Leah studied the beautiful blond, blue-eyed woman in the short, silver lamé dress.

"Hi, Elise," Jeremy said with a smile. "Leah, this is Elise Johnson. She's working with me on a fund-raiser to enlarge the emergency room at Whitehorn Memorial Hospital."

Leah hardly had time to acknowledge the introduction before Elise put her hand on Jeremy's shoulder and said to Leah, "You don't mind, do you?"

Leah's intimate evening with Jeremy suddenly seemed less so, and she *did* mind the woman intruding. But her good manners made her say, "Of course not. I wouldn't want to monopolize him." Feeling insecure, afraid she would see a warmth she didn't want to see in Jeremy's eyes as he danced with Elise, she turned away and headed for the punch bowl. Trying to keep her mind off of the prickly feelings she was experiencing, she became involved in a conversation with Melissa North, the owner of the Hip Hop, complimenting her on the food and the New Year's Eve atmosphere.

It seemed like a very long time later when Jeremy returned to her side.

Melissa excused herself and headed for the kitchen.

Dropping his arm around Leah's shoulders, Jeremy asked, "Would you like to dance again?"

Unbearably unsettled, Leah moved away from him on the pretense of setting down her cup. "Maybe you'd rather dance with some of the other women here."

He took hold of Leah's shoulder and nudged her around to face him. "I'm asking *you* to dance."

"I don't want you to feel obligated."

"What's wrong, Leah?"

"Nothing," she said a little too quickly.

Now he tipped her chin up. "Do I see a hint of the green-eyed monster in those beautiful dark brown eyes?" he asked with a smile.

"Elise is a sophisticated woman," she remarked, as if that explained it all.

"Elise is a woman who has a head for figures and for public relations techniques. I've worked with her. I've never dated her. I don't *want* to date her. You're the woman I want in my arms on that dance floor and other places. Am I making myself clear?"

Her cheeks grew hot. "Yes."

Taking her hand, he tugged her to an empty space near the jukebox, then took her into his arms. But he didn't bother with the customary dance position. He locked his hands at her waist, and her arms had no place to go but around his neck. Bringing her closer to him, he said, "Look up."

When she did, she spotted a ball of mistletoe. His lips came down on hers hard, his tongue delved into her mouth, and she forgot they were standing in the middle of a party. When he broke the kiss, she looked around to see if anyone had noticed. But the other couples around them were dancing, lost in their own celebrations of the New Year. Jeremy kissed her again with lingering sweetness, and then she laid her head on his chest, moving with him to the music, listening to the beat of his heart.

She couldn't wait until they went home tonight and could spend some time alone.

Chapter Six

Snow fell lightly as Jeremy pulled up behind Leah's van in front of her house. "Are you tired?" he asked, knowing she probably was, hoping she'd invite him to stay anyway.

"I managed a nap with the babies this afternoon so I'd be awake tonight."

Her soft voice in the interior of the dark car was as arousing as the thought of spending the night with her.

Climbing out of the Jeep, Jeremy went around to Leah's door before she opened it. Giving her a hand, he helped her out, then scooped her up into his arms. "The sidewalk's slippery. I don't want you to fall."

She didn't argue with him but tightened her arms

around his neck. He didn't hurry to carry her to the porch. There was an awesome quality about the night—the black sky, the softly falling snow, the silence.

"I had a lovely time tonight," Leah said.

"It was a great start to a new year," he agreed.

When the clock had struck midnight at the Hip Hop, he'd taken Leah into his arms and kissed her deeply, longing for a future with her, longing for the family he'd never had. Now as she looked up at him and snowflakes nestled in her beautiful black hair, he kissed her again with enough fervor to tell her he wanted to stay the night. He just wanted to *be* with her and his children.

After he set her down on the porch, she took her keys from her pocket and opened the door.

Bessie was curled up on the sofa reading by the lamp on the end table. "Did you have a good time?" she asked.

"We had a great time," Jeremy answered. "How were the twins?"

Rising from the sofa, Bessie picked up her coat. "They were just fine. Adam woke up at midnight as if he wanted to celebrate the new year with me. So I fed him and settled him down again. Brooke's been sleeping since eleven."

As if on cue, a cry came from the bedroom. It started slowly, then became louder.

"That's Brooke now," Leah said with a smile. She crossed to Bessie and gave her a hug. "Thank you so much for staying with them."

"Any time. You know that. Go on now. Take care of her before she wakes Adam."

After Leah went into the bedroom, Jeremy helped Bessie on with her coat and walked her to the door. When he wished her a happy new year and good night, she didn't comment his staying, but took it as a matter of course.

He was hoping Leah would, too. Actually, he was hoping he could convince Leah and the twins to move in with *him*.

Going to the bedroom doorway, he looked inside. Leah was rocking Brooke, humming softly to her. The floor light cast a pale glow on them both, and the tableau made his chest tighten. Leah was absorbed with nurturing her daughter, and he decided not to disturb her. He'd wait in the living room until she was finished.

Seeing the newspaper on the coffee table, he took off his suit coat, tugged down his tie and settled on the sofa. But thinking about Leah, maybe holding her in his arms for the night, kept him distracted. He glanced over the paper quickly. Noticing the crossword puzzle, he decided focused concentration might keep him occupied until Leah was finished in the bedroom. But he needed something to write with. He remembered Leah had a kitchen drawer that held notepaper and pens. He went into the kitchen and opened the drawer farthest from the sink. He was removing a ballpoint when his finger caught on an envelope. He glanced at it. It was from the Museum of History Through the Ages in Washington, D.C.

As he picked up the envelope, he saw the letter lying beneath it. It was addressed to Leah, and before he thought better of it, he read the first paragraph.

His stomach clenched.

All Leah had to do was call that number after the new year and she'd have a job interview in Washington, D.C. Exactly what she wanted. Exactly what she'd always dreamed of. Exactly what her mother had wanted for her.

Why hadn't she told him?

He remembered her saying she'd sent out résumés, but she'd never mentioned receiving replies. Why? Did she want to sneak the twins away so he couldn't convince her to stay? Or did she want to make sure she had the job before she told him about it?

Fury arose inside Jeremy. He'd thought they were getting closer. He'd thought marriage was in their future. He'd thought they could become a family. But apparently Leah was making other plans. Faced with the concrete possibility of Leah leaving Montana, Jeremy realized just how many plans *he'd* been making in his head. He'd already decided he could fence in his backyard, put in a jungle gym and swing set, easily give Adam and Brooke their own rooms. But most of all, he'd been imagining Leah in his home, relaxing with him in the living room, sharing his bed. It was a dream, a dream she apparently didn't want to share.

He paced her living room, the letter still in his hand. When Leah finally emerged from the bedroom, she saw it, and stopped a good two feet away from him.

"Are your bags already packed?" he asked cynically, feeling foolish for weaving a dream on his own.

"Of course not. I can't even make an appointment until after the new year."

"But you *do* intend to make it?"

"It's a terrific opportunity, Jeremy. It's what I've always wanted."

"I thought what you wanted might have changed. You have babies to care for now, Leah. How are you going to do that and work at the same time?"

Her chin lifted. "Lots of women do it."

"Maybe so, but that doesn't mean it's best for them or their kids."

"Single mothers don't have any choice."

"Maybe they don't, but you do. You don't have to be a single mother. I proposed marriage, remember?"

Her eyes were big and sad. "I remember. But just why *did* you propose marriage? Because that's what's best for the twins? That's what's best for you? What about me? What about *my* life? Maybe I want more than a marriage of convenience."

Her words slid over his anger and he simply caught their essence. "When you have children, you have to stop putting yourself first. Together we could give our twins the life they deserve."

"What about the life *we* deserve?" she asked, looking hurt, and he didn't understand why.

"We could have a good life," he exploded, feeling her slipping away, feeling the future he wanted slipping away.

"Maybe *you* could have a good life, but I want more than being a replacement for the wife you lost. I want more for Brooke and Adam than for them to fill the hole in your life left by your unborn child."

Leah's accusations shocked him, and he lashed out. "You talk about the dreams your mother had for you, and not wanting her sacrifices to be in vain. I think your motives are a lot less noble than that. Maybe you don't want to be reminded of your roots, maybe you'd rather forget your heritage, maybe you just want to be a part of a bigger world where everybody is the same. But leaving the res and Whitehorn isn't going to change who you are."

"You have no right—"

"I *do* have rights, Leah. I went to Gil Brown the first time to set up trust funds, but maybe I'll be seeing him soon for another reason entirely."

Tears came to her eyes. "You said the twins belong with me."

"They do. But you're not going to cut me out of their lives. I won't take them away from you, but I want to make sure you can never take them away from me, either."

He couldn't handle the shocked look on her face, the hurt caused by the things he'd said. Most of all, he couldn't stand the knowledge that she didn't want him, that she could walk away so easily. Snatching up his suit coat, he tossed it over his arm, and then he closed the door behind him and didn't look back.

Because if he looked back, he'd have to face the kind of pain he'd felt after Gwen and his child died.

He didn't want to face that pain ever again.

On New Year's Day, Leah found herself crying as she cared for Brooke and Adam, crying as she poured out what had happened on New Year's Eve to Bessie over a cup of tea, and crying as she lay awake that night staring into the dark, thinking about Jeremy, holding on to her love for him, wishing he loved her, too. But it was so very obvious that he didn't. He couldn't have said what he had if he did.

She wasn't running away from who she was; she didn't want to run at all. If Jeremy felt more than desire, more than responsibility for his children, they'd have a place to start. But he'd spoken as if she and the twins were just a package deal he was willing to accept. She wanted a marriage based on love, and she wouldn't settle for less. If she did, she'd not only hurt herself, but she'd hurt Brooke and Adam. They needed so much more than a roof over their heads and a nice house and a college education. They needed parents who would love them for who they were, every day of their lives. She and Jeremy could do that separately; she wasn't sure they could do it together. If he had no feelings for her except desire, then she *was* simply a replacement, and she wouldn't be that.

Even though she loved him to the depths of her being,

When Jeremy didn't call her on New Year's Day or the next, she knew she had to build her life as she'd planned to do when she'd found out she was pregnant—without him. Monday morning, taking the time zones into consideration, she called Washington, D.C.

Monday evening, the wind beat against the old miner's hut in the Crazy Mountains. Dillon Pierce threw an empty wooden bucket across the room with an oath and watched it bounce off the wall. He'd been shut up here since Willie Sparks had screwed up and let their million-dollar kid escape. He was tired of lugging water from the creek, tired of being afraid to go near a town, tired of sleeping on a bunk that was practically as hard as the ground. If only they could find out if the kid had fingered them yet...

Dillon glanced at the snake tattoo on his forearm. She'd seen that...she'd seen their faces...

The sound of a truck bumping up the snow-covered, rutted logging road put Dillon on guard. He raked his black hair out of his eyes and peered through the small window. It was Willie.

When the battered door opened, Dillon muttered, "It's about time you got back here with food. I'm starving."

"It was worth the wait," Willie said with a smirk. "Wait till you see what I got."

Besides the bag of groceries in his arm, Willie

held up a newspaper. "I found it in a trash bin. Check out the front page."

Dillon snatched the paper from Willie and sat in the chair closest to the potbellied stove. The headline on the front page of the *Whitehorn Journal* snagged his attention. Kidnapping Gone Awry.

"We had the wrong kid?" he exploded after he'd skimmed the article.

"Looks that way," Willie answered as he set the bag on the table. "The good part is—she ain't told nobody nothin' yet. She can't talk. Or *won't* talk. People at the Hip Hop are gabbin' up a storm about it."

"You went to the Hip Hop?"

"After I saw the paper, I figured, why shouldn't I? That's the place to find out what's happening. And I did. The kid we had, Sara Mitchell, ain't peeped a word since they found her. You tellin' her you'd kill her and her family if she ever told what we looked like must have worked!"

"Must have," Dillon agreed.

"So let's get the hell out of here," Willie suggested. "We can drive down to Texas, maybe disappear into Mexico."

"Mexico? Are you nuts? We've got to get this kid and make sure she never identifies us."

"You don't mean—"

"Oh, yes, I do. If we eliminate her, we can go anywhere we want. I'm not running the rest of my life."

"I don't know…"

"If you're not with me, you get the hell out of

here now, Willie. But without my truck. And without the little bit of money I have stashed.''

Willie gave Dillon a lost look as if he had no idea how to move on alone.

''Well?'' Dillon pressed.

''All right. I'll help you. But I won't hurt her. Understand?''

One thing Dillon had learned about Willie Sparks—he did what he was told. ''Yeah, I understand. Now let's eat. I'm starved.'' He unloaded the groceries, hoping feeding his stomach would help him come up with a plan—a plan to set them free.

Jeremy was grabbing a quick sandwich at his desk on Tuesday afternoon when his receptionist buzzed him. ''There's a Bessie Whitecloud here to see you,'' she said.

Jeremy froze. What if something had happened to Leah? What if something was wrong with the twins? Closing his eyes, he tried to stuff the worry. He'd told himself he'd needed time to think; he'd told himself he had to stop making Leah, Brooke and Adam the center of his world; he'd told himself he was going to lose them, and he'd better get used to it.

''Send her back,'' he said curtly.

Dumping the remainder of his sandwich into the trash can, he opened his office door and waited until Bessie appeared, then went back inside and sat behind his desk.

She came in and asked, ''Do you have a few minutes?''

He made a point of checking his watch. "About five, then the waiting room will start filling with patients."

"Five might be all I need if you're smart enough to listen to me."

Bessie's tone was scolding and motherly, and he frowned. "Look, if this is about Leah, she and I said everything we had to say."

"This *is* about Leah, and I don't think the two of you have *begun* to say everything you should say. Leah had an hour-long conversation yesterday with the personnel director from the museum in Washington. It looks as if they want to interview her pretty badly as soon as possible. They haven't set up interviews with anyone else because they want to meet her first."

When Jeremy kept silent, Bessie went on. "They're offering her an all-expense-paid trip. She's taking the twins, and I'm going along to help. We're flying to D.C. on Thursday."

He still remained silent.

Shaking her head impatiently, Bessie asked, "Do you want her to take this job and move to Washington?"

"Obviously, Leah *wants* to move," he retorted, not thinking about what *he* wanted because it was too painful.

"You're acting like a man who's already lost and has no desire to fight."

He stood, unable to restrain the emotions that had been rioting since New Year's Eve. "What would

I be fighting for, Bessie? A marriage Leah doesn't want? A life she doesn't want?''

"Have you really ever *asked* Leah what she wants?'' Bessie's gaze held his and wouldn't let go.

"She's made it clear,'' he muttered.

"I don't think she has. She told you what she wanted before she came back here to take care of her mother. She told you what she wanted before she met you, before she had the twins. She's an independent young woman, Jeremy. She has to take care of herself and her babies. This job in Washington, D.C., would give her the best opportunity to do that. But that isn't necessarily what her heart desires.''

"And you think her heart's desire has something to do with me?'' He gave a humorless laugh. "Well, you're wrong. She thinks I want her and the twins to replace the family I lost.''

Silence again stretched between them until Bessie said, "Leah can only see what you let her see. Have you ever given her a reason to want to stay? Have you ever told her that she's *not* a replacement? Think about it, Jeremy. Think about what Leah means to your life, and then you decide if you want her to fly out of here on Thursday.''

Without waiting for a reaction or a response, Bessie left his office. Jeremy could hear her footsteps going down the hall as he sank into his swivel chair.

Think about what Leah meant to his life? That would only cause the pain he was trying to avoid.

Still, in spite of himself, he remembered the first

time he'd met Leah when she'd come into the clinic on the res. It had been last March. There had been a foot of snow on the ground, and she'd come in wearing boots and her parka, her cheeks red. When she'd let down her hood and he'd seen that glorious black hair of hers, looked into her deep brown eyes, he'd felt a soul-stirring pull. Over the month he'd cared for her mother, he'd defied that pull…until that one night when Leah had needed his arms around her, needed to know she wasn't alone.

He'd understood her grief better than anyone could, though he hadn't told her that then. But maybe she'd felt it. Maybe that's what had drawn them together. Although he'd thought Leah had left Whitehorn, she'd changed his world that night. Afterward he had felt more alive, more cognizant of everything around him. And when he'd found her by the side of the road and delivered their twins, he'd glimpsed the future they could have together.

He couldn't close his eyes at night without thinking about her…without seeing her. When he awoke in the morning, he wondered what she was doing and couldn't wait until he'd finished rounds or had seen all his patients so he could call her or stop by. She filled his thoughts, stirred his imagination, aroused his desire until he felt like a powerful man, ten feet tall, able to do anything. He didn't see her and the twins as a package deal. He saw Leah for who she was, and he—

He loved her.

Good Lord, how had he missed it? How had he not seen it? How could he have denied it?

It was simple, really. He'd been blind to his growing feelings for her because he hadn't wanted to take the risk of loving and possibly losing again. He hadn't wanted to admit he *could* love again. He'd told himself he was going to convince her to stay for the sake of the twins. But he wanted Leah to stay for *his* sake.

He loved her!

Because he hadn't been able to admit it to himself or to her, she thought she was simply convenient. She'd even told him on New Year's Eve that she didn't want a marriage of convenience. But it hadn't sunk in because he'd been too angry and hurt to hear it.

When he'd lashed out at her that night, he'd probably destroyed any trust that had built between them. How could she trust him when she didn't know how he felt, when he'd never told her she'd become the sun in his life, his reason for looking forward to each new day?

When she had accused him of thinking of her as a replacement, maybe it had hit a little too close to home. He had seen her and the twins as something that could fill his life with everything he'd lost. But she wouldn't be a substitute for Gwen; she wouldn't be a wife for the sake of his needing a wife.

She was Leah—special, courageous...

She'd had the courage to turn down his offer of marriage because it had been made for convenience's sake rather than out of love. And if he told her he loved her now...

That was a risk he'd have to take—if he wanted

to be fully alive again, if he wanted to have a future with Leah. Somehow, he'd make her believe him.

It was almost eight o'clock when Jeremy finally finished his rounds at the hospital. This afternoon he'd wanted to rush to Leah right away. But he'd needed time to think about what to say to her. He'd needed time to finish his work for the day, so if she accepted his proposal, he could stay with her to-night. All afternoon he'd concentrated on patients, but in between he'd worried about Leah's reac-tion—if she would believe what he had to say.

When he pulled up in front of her house, he switched off the ignition and took a deep breath, knowing this was the most important moment of his life.

As he went to the porch, he could see a lamp glowing in the living room. He knocked and waited.

When Leah opened the door, she looked sur-prised, and then guarded.

"Can I come in?" he asked.

Stepping back, she let him inside. "Adam and Brooke are sleeping," she said.

"I came to see you."

Her eyes widened, and he wished he could wipe the wariness from them and take her in his arms. Instead, he unsnapped his jacket, took it off and tossed it over the chair as he'd done so many times in the past few weeks. Leah stood there watching him, looking as if she were ready to grab the twins and run at a moment's notice. He'd done this to her…to them.

"I don't know where to start," he said honestly.

"What are you going to do about Brooke and Adam?"

She looked like a lioness ready to fight for her cubs, and he admired that about her, along with everything else. "I don't want to talk about Brooke and Adam. I want to talk about you and me."

Her expression didn't change, and he realized she'd put her defenses firmly in place. There was only one way to break through them. He had to lay everything on the line. "I love you, Leah, and I want to marry you." He rushed on. "I'm sorry if I gave you the impression that you and the twins would be replacements. Yes, you'd fill a gaping hole in my life, but you and Adam and Brooke are so much more important than that. I want to marry you because I love *you*. I want to spend my life with you because there's no one else I can imagine spending it with. And I want to be more than a father. I want to be your husband. I want you to walk with me through snow and sunshine. I want you to be my partner."

Taking her hands in his, he went on. "If you have any doubts, if you think I'm only doing this because of Brooke and Adam, I promise you that isn't true. I will spend the rest of my life proving to you that I love you. Can you forgive what I said on New Year's Eve? Can you believe me?"

Tears welled up in Leah's eyes, and one rolled down her cheek. He was afraid she was crying because he'd destroyed her feelings for him. He was afraid...

"Oh, Jeremy. I love you, too. I—"

Realizing she wasn't crying from sadness, but possibly from joy, he didn't wait for her to finish, but gathered her into his arms and kissed her with the passion that always caught fire so easily between them. When she wrapped her arms around his neck, she kissed him back as fervently as he kissed her. And he knew she wanted him in her life as much as he wanted her in his.

Reluctantly, he pulled away, but held her tightly. "Will you marry me?"

Her smile was sweet and tender and loving. "Yes, I'll marry you."

But he still had a worry to lay to rest. "What about the interview? What about your dream of working in New York or Washington? If that's what you really want..."

Resting a slender hand on each of his shoulders, she leaned back to gaze into his eyes. "I love you, Jeremy, and I want to be your wife. My roots are here. Brooke's and Adam's roots are here. Maybe I can start working again at the Museum in Whitehorn—when Brooke and Adam don't need me quite as much."

"But will that be enough?" he asked.

She nodded, then stood on tiptoe to kiss him again. After his lips caressed hers, after his tongue mated with hers, after his heart raced with desire and all the possibilities for the future, he ended the kiss to say, "Maybe we'll both want to explore New York or Washington someday. Maybe we'll both want to show Brooke and Adam more than Whitehorn. We can do that, too."

"We'll decide together," she said softly.

"Together," he agreed, then enfolded her in his arms again, filled with thanks and gratitude that he'd found her and she'd found him. And together they'd found their future.

Leah awakened in the dark, smiling. Jeremy's strong arms were wrapped around her, his broad chest warmed her back, his jaw rested on the top of her head. When he'd asked to come in earlier, she'd prepared herself for the worst. She'd been miserable thinking about a life apart from him. But after he'd gazed at her with such sincerity in his green eyes and told her he loved her, told her he wanted to spend his life with her, she'd known deep in her soul he was telling the truth. Jeremy had always told her the truth.

"Are you awake?" he whispered.

She turned under the covers to face him. Although they couldn't consummate their love in the physical sense, they had touched and kissed and talked and held each other, creating bonds that could never be broken.

"I like having you hold me while I sleep," she said.

Taking her hand, he brought it to his cheek and kissed her palm. "I love holding you. I love being here with you."

Moonlight glowed through the window, and she could see a question in his eyes. "What?" she asked.

"When can we get married?"

"When would you like to get married?"

He tucked her hand against his chest. "As soon as we can arrange it. Saturday, maybe? Or is that too soon? Do you need more time?"

She slid a little closer to him until their noses almost brushed. "I don't need more time. But I would like to get married here on the res—in the church we visited on Christmas."

"I'd like that, too." After a pause, he asked, "Are you ready to leave the res? Do you *want* to come live with me? We could find a new house somewhere else."

"I like your house, Jeremy. It doesn't matter where we live. I've discovered something over the past few weeks. Home isn't necessarily a place. For me now, home is you, and with you is where I belong. We can rent this house to someone who needs it, someone who can take care of it, the way my grandmother and my mother did."

Wrapping his arms around her, he rubbed her nose with his. "Do you know how special you are?"

"I know how special *we* are."

Jeremy kissed Leah's cheek and then her temple and then her lips, sealing their love, sealing their commitment, sealing their happily ever after.

*   *   *   *   *

MONTANA MAVERICKS

Big Sky Brides

Legendary love comes to Whitehorn, Montana, once more as beloved authors

Christine Rimmer, Jennifer Greene and Cheryl St.John

present three brand-new stories in this exciting anthology!

Meet the Brennan women:
SUZANNA, DIANA and ISABELLE

Strong-willed beauties who find unexpected love in these irresistible marriage of covnenience stories.

Don't miss
MONTANA MAVERICKS: BIG SKY BRIDES
On sale in February 2000,
only from Silhouette Books!

Available at your favorite retail outlet.

Visit us at www.romance.net PSMMBSB

If you enjoyed what you just read,
then we've got an offer you can't resist!

Take 2 bestselling love stories FREE!

Plus get a FREE surprise gift!

Clip this page and mail it to Silhouette Reader Service™

IN U.S.A.	**IN CANADA**
3010 Walden Ave.	P.O. Box 609
P.O. Box 1867	Fort Erie, Ontario
Buffalo, N.Y. 14240-1867	L2A 5X3

YES! Please send me 2 free Silhouette Special Edition® novels and my free surprise gift. Then send me 6 brand-new novels every month, which I will receive months before they're available in stores. In the U.S.A., bill me at the bargain price of $3.57 plus 25¢ delivery per book and applicable sales tax, if any*. In Canada, bill me at the bargain price of $3.96 plus 25¢ delivery per book and applicable taxes**. That's the complete price and a savings of over 10% off the cover prices—what a great deal! I understand that accepting the 2 free books and gift places me under no obligation ever to buy any books. I can always return a shipment and cancel at any time. Even if I never buy another book from Silhouette, the 2 free books and gift are mine to keep forever. So why not take us up on our invitation. You'll be glad you did!

235 SEN CNFD
335 SEN CNFE

Name _____ (PLEASE PRINT)

Address _____ Apt.#

City _____ State/Prov. _____ Zip/Postal Code

* Terms and prices subject to change without notice. Sales tax applicable in N.Y.
** Canadian residents will be charged applicable provincial taxes and GST.
   All orders subject to approval. Offer limited to one per household.
® are registered trademarks of Harlequin Enterprises Limited.

SPED99   ©1998 Harlequin Enterprises Limited

**Start celebrating Silhouette's 20th anniversary
with these 4 special titles by
New York Times bestselling authors**

Fire and Rain
by Elizabeth Lowell

King of the Castle
by Heather Graham Pozzessere

State Secrets
by Linda Lael Miller

Paint Me Rainbows
by Fern Michaels

On sale in December 1999

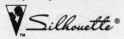

Montana Mavericks™

Return to Whitehorn

Look for these bold new stories set in beloved Whitehorn, Montana!

CINDERELLA'S BIG SKY GROOM by Christine Rimmer
On sale October 1999 (Special Edition #1280)
A prim schoolteacher pretends an engagement
to the town's most confirmed bachelor!

A MONTANA MAVERICKS CHRISTMAS
On sale November 1999 (Special Edition #1286)
A two-in-one volume containing
two brand-new stories:

"Married in Whitehorn" by Susan Mallery
and
"Born in Whitehorn" by Karen Hughes

A FAMILY HOMECOMING by Laurie Paige
On sale December 1999 (Special Edition #1292)
A father returns home to guard his wife and child—
and finds his heart once more.

*Don't miss these books, only from
Silhouette Special Edition.*

Look for the next **MONTANA MAVERICKS** tale, by
Jackie Merritt, on sale in Special Edition May 2000.
And get ready for
MONTANA MAVERICKS: Wed in Whitehorn,
a new twelve-book series coming from Silhouette Books
on sale June 2000!

Available at your favorite retail outlet.

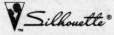

Silhouette®

Visit us at www.romance.net

Celebrate Silhouette's 20th Anniversary

With beloved authors, exciting new miniseries and special keepsake collections, **plus** the chance to enter our 20th anniversary contest, in which one lucky reader wins the trip of a lifetime!

Take a look at who's celebrating with us:

DIANA PALMER

April 2000: SOLDIERS OF FORTUNE
May 2000 in Silhouette Romance: *Mercenary's Woman*

NORA ROBERTS

May 2000: IRISH HEARTS, the 2-in-1 keepsake collection
June 2000 in Special Edition: *Irish Rebel*

LINDA HOWARD

July 2000: MACKENZIE'S MISSION
August 2000 in Intimate Moments: *A Game of Chance*

ANNETTE BROADRICK

October 2000: a special keepsake collection, plus a brand-new title in
November 2000 in Desire

Available at your favorite retail outlet.

Where love comes alive™

EXTRA! EXTRA!

**The book all your favorite authors
are raving about is finally here!**

**The 1999 Harlequin and Silhouette
coupon book.**

Each page is alive with savings that can't be beat!

**Getting this incredible coupon book is
as easy as 1, 2, 3.**

1. During the months of November and December 1999 buy any 2 Harlequin or Silhouette books.

2. Send us your name, address and 2 proofs of purchase (cash receipt) to the address below.

3. Harlequin will send you a coupon book worth $10.00 off future purchases of Harlequin or Silhouette books in 2000.

Send us 3 cash register receipts as proofs of purchase and we will send you 2 coupon books worth a total saving of $20.00 (limit of 2 coupon books per customer).

Saving money has never been this easy.

Please allow 4-6 weeks for delivery. Offer expires December 31, 1999.
